The Old Orange Tree

THE OLD ORANGE TREE

Philip Robinson

SECOND EDITION

ULSTER-SCOTS ACADEMY PRESS

First published by Ullans Press, 2009

Second edition by the Ulster-Scots Academy Press, 2021

Also by the same author:

Esther, Quaen o tha Ulidian Pechts (1997)
Fergus an tha Stane o Destinie (1999)
Alang tha Shore (2006)
Oul Licht, New Licht (2009)
Wake the Tribe o Dan (Second edition, 2020)
The Back Streets o the Claw (Second edition, 2021)
The Man frae the Ministry (Second edition, 2021)

ISBN 978-1-8384549-2-0

For Amy, Beth and Fergus

Note: The historical quotations and 17th century characters in this novel are factual (relating to Greyabbey, County Down), but the modern characters, buildings and events of Kirkreeba are purely fictional.

CONTENTS

CONTENTS

Chapter 1

Next Stop China

"Young Samuel Hamilton [John Steinbeck's grandfather] *came from the north of Ireland and so did his wife. He was the son of small farmers, neither rich nor poor, who had lived on one landhold for many hundreds of years.*

Samuel and Liza Hamilton got all of their children raised and well towards adulthood before the turn of the century ... Samuel sunk well after well and could not find water on his own land.

'I'll dig your wells for you if I have to drive my rig to the black centre of the earth. I'll squeeze water out like the juice of an orange.'"

John Steinbeck *East of Eden*

'The world,' said Esther Hamilton to her two youngest children, 'isnae perfect roon, but mair the shape o an orange.' She held the treat in her hand up in front of their faces, knowing that a child always learns best when waiting like a clever pup for its reward. Still holding the orange up like a floating planet above the heads of her captivated audience, she produced a knitting needle from the knife box on the wall and plunged it through. 'And if yer granda dug a wal, an kep on diggin, – he would come oot the ither side o the world, like *that!*'

'Naw if he dug himsel intae hell first,' said Samuel innocently.

'Well, that's enough o that,' said Esther, reaching again into the knife box for a sharp knife to cut the orange in two halves. Samuel's sharp eyes picked out the bigger half, but his mother was ahead of him. She handed the big bit to Elsie and the other to Samuel.

'What do you say, Samuel?' she said, pulling it back out of his grabbing reach til he would show his good manners.

'The world,' Samuel said, 'is ill divid.'

On the other side of the world, Samuel Hamilton was to dig many a well in what became known as Steinbeck country, east of California's Monterey. And then he became a granda himself. That was all a hundred years or so back, but there are still traces of them (wells and Hamilton descendants), if you know where to look. One such well survives today in a long valley plain between the north Californian mountain ranges, but its digger and its Scotch-Irish connections are no longer remembered. Without this well there would have been nothing built for three miles along the road into the nearest oasis town of Orange Grove. As it stands with the well now a hundred years old, its only legacy is a run-down house and a solitary tree clinging almost hopelessly to the site of the old well. The timber shack was in such bad repair that a single blow from a repairing hammer might easily flatten the lot. The old tree had seen better days too, but at daybreak boasted a cock and a roost for some chickens in its branches. Between and around these relics there was a scattering of clutter – a warning that the site wasn't completely abandoned.

The King homestead was in no imminent danger of repair, for Joseph King and his son Joel were a perfect match for each other and the shack. But they were out early this Monday morning from first light. They had settled back down from the exertions of getting out of their stinking warm beds, into a roadside hut made of old fruit packing cases. Their half-closed eyes were waiting for any swirl of dust that might signal passing trade, for their only apparent source of income was a roadside fruit stall. The only apparent source of fruit was the old arthritic orange tree crouching motionless by the well.

A pick-up truck with dirt-covered writing on its side pulled off the road opposite and swung round to face back into Orange Grove. Nobody stirred from the shelter or from the truck until the dust settled. Then a tall man in rough working denims and clean, short-sleeved shirt jumped down from the driver's seat, using the door as a swing and leaving it open behind him in the swelling heat. He walked over towards the house as if he owned the place. But he was too clean and full of purpose to look like he belonged. In the still rising heat, there wasn't even a creak from the joints of the tree. A hen scraiched down from its branches and another ran out from under a make-shift nest box that had a car door for a roof.

'She'll be out in a minute,' a voice snarled from inside the roadside shelter, back near the fruit stall. Joseph King emerged from its shade and stood as a wolf might eye its prey, waiting for the man to come back towards him.

'Eggs?'

Pat Mahood spoke with the confidence of a man that knew no fear. He could be just as curt and as hard as the next man. Joseph turned back and his son's hand reached out a light brown re-used paper bag. 'Four,' he replied without offering Pat the bag.

'Gimme the lot an' three oranges.'

'A dollar fifty.'

It was a ritual dance, for the both men knew that the last thing Pat Mahood needed to do was to drive out of Orange Grove to buy oranges, or fruit of any kind. And they both knew that none of the fruit on Joseph King's stall came from his own trees. This exchange was a daily run out for Pat, as he called in at the King's place for what he said was his mother's crazy notion of fresh eggs. He put the bag in the truck and reached out another identical brown bag with the weekend's unused bread in it. 'For the hens,' he muttered as he handed it over to Joseph's ungrateful snatch. They both knew the hens would probably be lucky to get even a few crusts, but the bread had to be treated as if it was waste. Joseph could only take it if it didn't look like a hand-out, and he was doing the pest a favour even accepting it. And it had to be offered by Pat only after his money had been handed over for the eggs.

Anna came out from the house once she saw the transactions were complete. She was barely eighteen, but was rapidly becoming the double of her Mexican mother, just like she had looked when she died at the age of twenty-seven. Pat didn't acknowledge Anna when the young girl ran past behind him towards the truck with her head down.

'Mind you an' get back 'fore six, Miss,' barked Joseph at his daughter as she climbed into the passenger seat. 'Yes sir,' she said, keeping her head down.

Joseph spat crudely near Pat's feet to remind him whose territory he was on. Pat ignored it, on the outside at least, and smiled as he nodded towards the shelter. 'Joel want a ride into town too?'

'Wanna hitch a ride into town, boy?' Joseph said over his shoulder.

'Naw.'

Joseph smiled scornfully out of one side of his mouth to register a small victory. Pat smiled back, shrugged his shoulders and left without a 'thank-you,' a wave or a 'have a nice day' from either party.

'Don't worry, ye'll get to work 'fore yer start time,' Pat said to his nervous passenger. 'OK?' He smiled his assurance, and turned on the radio with his long brown right hand. She had to be there ten minutes before her official start time, which began when the coffee shop opened, but Anna felt completely safe in Pat's hands.

'Thanks Mr. Mahood,' Anna smiled back with her mouth and eyes as she gave a happy sigh and lifted her head up and back. There was some thing about her home situation that made Pat suspicious. And back at the well Joseph King knew that Pat sensed it.

Like many a small respectable town on the west coast of America, Orange Grove had a heart but no centre. Magill's bookstore for new and used books, where Pat had to call after dropping Anna at her work, was at the out-of-town end of Main Street. At the other end of Main Street was an open grass area where a bulbous, alloy water tower on tubular legs proclaimed the settlement's name in big white letters above the height of the trees. This well in the sky was the nearest thing to a central point in the town.

· · · · · · · · · ·

David Magill had a nagging doubt about his livelihood in that bookstore. It was at the centre of his life, but one reservation kept it from being the closest thing to his heart. He resented the fact that his wife Kay owned the premises. She had been left her father's family store as a going concern and, to please David, she had set it up as a bookshop. And so, David's nagging thought went, she owned both it and him. Although he had lived in California since his early teens, David still carried some cultural baggage from the 'oul country.' His family had left east Ulster for a new life in the sun when he was still a child. At his own house, forty years on, he still planted his front and back yard out with beds and plants that reflected his childhood memory of what a garden should be like, but he did that without thinking.

He knew he missed the sense of being snugly enclosed in narrow streets by tall buildings, but there wasn't much he could do about that in the open tree-lined criss-crossing boulevards of Orange Grove. He preferred a shift-stick car to an automatic, and he liked to walk places rather than take the car when he was just going the length of the street. This morning, as always, he would walk the two blocks from home to the bookstore to open up. Kay would come in later in the car, and he would drive them both back home at 5.30 pm.

It was early Monday morning, and David detoured across the open grass square in front of the High School. It was just nice, not too hot yet. A man he half-knew was getting ready to paint the white woodwork of the bandstand in the centre of the green. 'Hi Dave,' the man smiled. David couldn't remember his name or where he lived. 'Hi,' he answered, smiling back as the man stretched up from his hunkers where he was squatting at his tins, 'Many out at your church yesterday?' He added. He wanted to show that he did recognise him, for he remembered that yesterday the painter had been standing outside the door of the American Baptist Church, with another man, as Dave had passed in the car. The twosome had been in white short-sleeved shirts, finishing a smoke and scanning the empty streets at about one minute off the advertised starting time on the church notice board. The man's smile dropped. 'The usual,' he said. 'Yeah,' David replied with an understanding sigh. As David walked on past the same corner and American Baptist church, he looked at the sign board. Now that could do with a lick of paint, he thought. The faded letters had the unconvincing and conflicting messages of 'Everyone Welcome' and 'Old Style Hymns.' He crossed the street to avoid his mother's church door. Orange Grove Presbyterian was the biggest of a dozen or so churches in the town, and in its hall at the back was where Kay's 'Crossroads Fellowship' crowd met. All sorts, all ages, all happy and clapping, guitars and mikes, with Kay at the centre of things as always. David breathed more easily as he turned into Main Street and dropped down a gear to a casual stroll.

'Hi, honey,' Kay breezed in to the bookstore, fumbling with bags and keys, and sticking her backside out to hold the spring-loaded door open. 'Any mail?'

But David didn't answer. He was in the back room, hoaking through a box of unsorted books he had bought 'blind' on Saturday just before closing up.

'There's just one I'd be interested in,' he had said on Saturday evening, picking out a standard paperback of John Steinbeck's. 'Three dollars,' he said, guessing the man just wanted to get rid of the lot, 'local interest I guess.' The man was a stranger and obviously didn't know. 'How much for the whole box then?' he appealed. 'Five dollars, at the most, I'll just have to dump most of them.' David had glimpsed straight away, as he was talking, an old hardback copy at the bottom of the pile. He had to force himself to ignore it, for to open it up and find it was a valuable first edition – and then offer next to nothing – would have been dishonest. And to make a better offer might have raised the man's suspicions. 'O.K.' the man had said, glad to be rid of the lot and David calmly dumped the box in the back as if he was glad to be rid of another non-customer.

'Hi, honey. Any mail today?' Kay repeated when she came into the back and saw David had just started to open up the mail pretending he hadn't heard her the first time. 'Just the usual,' he said, with the same air of resignation that the man painting the bandstand had voiced. The business accounts all were addressed to Mrs K. Magill, as the 'owner,' but Dave tried to ignore that and usually opened them all anyway. She opened his mail at home, and that was another thing he really didn't like. He often gave out his own private address as 'The Bookstore,' Main Street, so he could get to his own personal stuff first.

As Kay hung up her floppy, broad-rimmed hat on an old-fashioned hat-stand in the corner of the back room, she turned and cheerily patted David's shoulders from the back. 'Leave that honey till later. You just go and get your breakfast coffee.'

'Right,' Dave said, trying to sound reluctant, an act that was easy enough when he didn't want to be sent like the office junior to go down the street. But this morning in particular he did want his morning coffee break. 'Can you finish all this?' he questioned assertively. Kay always did the paperwork anyway. 'Sure, honey, you just run along.' Her answer irritated him again. He stood up and lifted the newspaper, put it in his left hand, lifted an unopened letter with a British stamp marked 'Private and Confidential,' and then used both to conceal the gem of a rare book from Saturday's box that he could hardly wait to inspect more closely. Just as he was nearly free, Kay added, 'once we get our own coffee counter and sit-out area built in here, we can just …' – she was off on her hobby-horse again.

'We'll see. At the coffee place they say that once we start selling coffee, Steinbeck's Coffee Shop will start selling books.'

'Tish! That's just George,' Kay said with a dismissive wave of her hand and an even more dismissive smile. David shook his head and took his private reading material out as if he was being dismissed himself. But Kay knew that pretended grumpiness look. She thought correctly that he was really quite excited inside. She thought wrongly that it was because he shared her cosy vision of how her bookshop could be a real success with more 'drop-in' facilities.

Steinbeck's Coffee Shop was just round the corner, but to David it was like another world. It was still early morning, and the sun wasn't yet so hot that the vine-covered canopy over the outside tables was an essential refuge. But the dappled, dancing light gave him a good, 'this is the life' sort of feeling. A large man with patterned shorts and sandals was sitting with an un-touched cappuccino in front of his newspaper. If he hadn't been sitting at David's favourite spot it would have been a heartsome sight. This was what it was all about. Reading for pleasure while relaxing and having a social coffee in inspiring surroundings – what more could a man want?

'What can I get you today, Mr. Magill? A muffin and large regular?' Anna King smiled and bounced on her toes as she welcomed David with teenage enthusiasm. She felt liberated with a whole day away from home in front of her.

'The usual, yes please, my dear.' David's eyes, old enough to be her father's, twinkled back at her. 'And over there,' he added seeing that his usual table had been freed.

'Yeah, Mr. Magill, you always like to sit beside the pretty flowers. Me too.'

Anna was right. What a pretty face she had. The tiered pots and tubs of busy lizzies hummed with bright cascading colours and some even sparkled where they had been just watered. Anna had gone over to clear and wipe the table, and pulled his seat back with a little mock curtsy and big broad Hispanic smile.

Steinbeck's Coffee shop was an institution in Orange Grove. A man with a white moustache came in and sat down at the next table. His long-haired dog flopped down wearily at his sandaled feet. He looked a bit like the overseer in the straw hat that had been painted on the wall mural opposite. It was an Orange plantation scene painted on the side wall of an otherwise un-attractive Fruit Packing and Storage Depot building. The high monolithic and brightly painted wall somehow made David feel comfortable and at home. The women picking oranges were all bright and smiling. One even looked like Anna. The scene of criss-crossing rows of Orange Trees which disappeared in two directions at the same time was like an exercise in order and perspective. It was a corner of paradise, sitting there. And as

Anna came back round the stem of the over-hanging vine, she seemed like an angel in the garden.

'Were you singing with the praise group again yesterday?' David asked Anna as he wiped a drip of coffee from his slightly greying and oversized moustache. If there was anything that might draw him into Crossroads on a Sunday morning it was that. But then he would have to watch over Kay's beaming face as she bobbed and clapped her mike-holding hands together in front of the line-up.

'Oh yes, were you there too, Mr. Magill?'

David shook his head in silence. He was slightly disappointed that she hadn't been actually looking out for him, or noticed his absence as usual. Carefully he put his unopened newspaper on the table beside his coffee. Then he opened the old hardback copy of his new trophy, *Of Mice and Men*. Yes! Its date of publication was 1937. And inside was written, 'To W. C. Brooks, from John Steinbeck.' A first edition Steinbeck inscribed by the author!

'Business going well?'

David hadn't heard George Hamilton, the owner of the coffee shop, come and sit down beside him. 'Sorry, did I make you jump?'

'No, George. I mean yeah. Business couldn't be better.'

George and David had a shared interest in Steinbeck as the only international literary icon to have a local connection. George saw his coffee shop as the cultural centre of Steinbeck Country, despite the real centre being a good hour's drive away. He had made it the rendezvous point for the local guided tour of the Steinbeck Heritage Trail. David was pleased that the cultural tourists would often stop at his bookshop for a browse and a paperback souvenir. And they always had a peep through the locked glass doors of his rare book collection.

'Here's one for your Steinbeck book club, George. It's an inscribed first edition, no less!'

'Where did you get that?' George said.

'Oh, I just found it among a job lot I got in through the trade …' His voice trailed off as he realised he wasn't quite telling the truth. He never engaged in polite conversation with callers wanting to sell off their house clearances. Nor asked their name. Then he wouldn't feel guilty when he made a gold strike like the one today.

'That must be worth hundreds.'

'*Hundreds?* Would you believe five or six *thousand!* Not bad for a day's work, eh George?' But George knew once it got into David's special collection in the store's First Editions case, it would never be parted with anyway. Just as well, for David's collection was rapidly becoming part of the heritage trail, especially when the book-man himself was around to share his enthusiasm with anyone that looked anywhere near that section of the store. The books in there could be examined on request, but they had no prices marked on them. Even if David decided to sell, he didn't want to broadcast their real value.

'Top up, Mr Magill?' Anna was back with her warm jug of coffee, and even warmer smile.

'Yeah. Why not.'

David had more private reading to do. He set the precious volume *Of Mice and Men* on the newspaper and folded the paper over it protectively. Then he took the envelope with the Air Mail sticker and British stamp out of his pocket. It had a solicitor's imprint. He recognised the lawyer's name as the firm that was handling the estate of his uncle Hugh. It was six months since the last letter came to inform him that he was the sole beneficiary of the estate of the late Hugh Magill, esquire, of the townland of Ballyneaster in Kirkreeba Parish. There were plenty of other Magill cousins back home, even in Kirkreeba, but this particular will and testament was the 'best laid scheme' of neither mouse nor man.

David's namesake and very distant ancestor, the 'Reverend' David Magill late curate of Kirkreeba and Westerkirk, had left his considerable estate in 1633 to his direct or nearest male descendants 'in perpetuity.' The history books tell the story of how his plantation laird had granted him the property as an inducement to settle under him in 1606 when he first brought him as his chaplain from Scotland. The Rev. Magill (sometimes McGill) then had everything tied up for his male heirs in a legal deed concocted by his own father, who had been Attorney to King James VI. The restrictive clauses prevented any future beneficiary disposing of the property and receiving any benefits other than occupancy and payment for the value of any improvements. So, like the legendary ferryman imprisoned by his duties until relieved by another victim, his uncle Hugh was replaced in a long line of Magill nominees by David as the newly-entrapped steward of some forgotten mission. He would be, if he took it up, little more than a land agent for his ancestors' estate. The first letter had even warned him that the estate may have a negative monetary value, but if so, the lawyer did assure him that the debts would not be considered personal liabilities.

At last, this was it. He hadn't told Kay anything about his inheritance notification. Not that he was being deliberately secretive, but he didn't know what was involved, or what his options were. At least, if it was all debt and duty, he could just sit tight in Orange Grove. They would hardly extradite him, an American citizen for the past forty years. And even if it was all good news, he was reared in the Scotch-Irish mould of westward pioneering, with no turning back when you hit the Pacific. But the real reason he hadn't told Kay was that he wanted to put the whole thing out of his mind – until he could see the devil in the detail.

And here it was. For the second time that morning he felt a thrill as he began to read. He skimmed over the key words, speed reading to get the basic plot. *'Be it kent til all men ... ye umquhile Hugh McGill ... all the lands, biggins, rents ... being situate and lyand in Easterton and Easterhill, alias Ballineaster ... '* David skipped this til he got to the solicitor's summary, *'Please sign and return ... claim ... absolute ownership for your entire life ... the late Hugh Magill's dwelling house, offices, gardens and lands in Kirkreeba as outlined on the attached map, including the premises known as the Orange Tree Tea Rooms adjacent to Kirkreeba Abbey.'* Well, well, thought David, 'The Orange Tree Tea Rooms!' He had forgotten the strange coincidence of name, for it was an old hostelry and the name had existed long before his family's flitting to Orange County, never mind his own settling down in Orange Grove.

When Kay and he were first married, they had taken a vacation touring Ireland and Scotland. They fitted in a quick visit to David's uncle Hugh, his father's cousin, to do a bit of family tree stuff. But that was years ago and he could barely remember the Tea Room. Auntie Liz looked after that side of things, and he wasn't sure he had even been inside. It was old-fashioned, if the sign outside advertising 'luncheons' and 'high teas' was anything to go by. The passing trade depended on visitors to the Abbey ruins. Its prime commercial site was presumably a legacy of Rev. Magill's original business, which was also dependent on visitors to the Abbey kirk.

But now, all of a sudden and with David just about to retire, he had such life-changing decisions to make. For all his supposed Scotch-Irish spirit, there wasn't much of a pioneer in him. Adventure to him was self-inflicted stress. The thought of serving tea in china cups in Kirkreeba was just about as attractive as the idea of working in a tea plantation in China. But then, he hadn't inherited property in China! And then there was Kay. For a fleeting moment he had imagined himself there, with young Anna King, running the Tea Room. But that was fantasy. He felt a double thrill at the thought of giving Kay an ultimatum she would never accept. But that was fantasy too, and there was no thrill in the real prospect of telling her.

Chapter 2

East of Eden

The Mochil Grei Abbei

...

Ther is a wel fair abbei
Of white monkes and of grei
Ther beth bowris and halles
Al of pasteiss beth the walles,
Of fleis, of fisse and rich met,
The likfullest that man mai et.
Fluren cakes beth the schingles alle
Of cherche, cloister, boure and halle
Ther is a cloister fair and light,
Brod and lang of sembli sight.

...

In the praer is a tre,
Swithe likful forto se.
The rote is gingeuir and galingale,
The siouns beth al sedwale,
Trie maces beth the flure,
The rind canel of swet odur,
The frute gilofre of gode smakke.

...

The yung monkes euch dai
Aftir met goth to plai.
Nis ther hauk no fule so swifte
Bettir fleing bi the lifte

Than the monkes heigh of mode,
With har sleuis and har hode.
Whan the abbot seeth ham flee,
That he holt for moch glee.
Ak natheless al ther amang,
He biddeth ham light to euesang.
The monkes lighteth noght adun
Ak furre fleeth in o randun.

Anon. *The Land of Cokaygne,* circa 1330

The men-folk of Kirkreeba were proud of their bowling club, for it had the most historic and beautiful setting of any green in the country. Towering over three sides like a backdrop to an epic movie were the grey stone ruins of the 12th century abbacy church and its monastic outbuildings – with the sheltered bowling-green slotted right in where the cloisters once were. The missing fourth side of the original cloisters had been the sleeping quarters of those lay monks who had worked the land 800 years back. Now the 'missing' lay brothers' dormitory was open to a boundary hedge separating the outside world from the holy site. There was a green-painted wooden door through an arch in the hedge with K.B.C. in small white letters painted at about eye-height by, or for, a small person. Outside the hedge was Sliddery Raa, a terrace of half-a-dozen old houses facing the green, and at their far gable, a timber club-house for the bowlers painted with the same green and white gloss. When the club house was opened, Councillor Hugh Magill had extravagantly proclaimed the Kirkreeba Bowling Club to have the best green and now the best club-house in the world. As far as the men that built the Abbacy all those years ago were concerned, Councillor Magill proclaimed, 'them masons that set oot the cloisters must hae knowed us bowlers were comin.'

The M'Clay brothers and their bed-ridden father lived

rent-free in the first house of Sliddery Raa, in return for their half-hereditary and half-official role as green-keepers. It was a relief when the twins took over, for old Ephie M'Clay had become too feeble in body and mind for this critical task. He used to water the green with a hose not only in the dry spells, but also in the pouring rain. 'Ye're daein a brave job, Ephie,' spectating wits would shout over the hedge through the downpour, 'but ye hae missed a bit behin ye.' Ephie was stunned when he realized that the young lads were making fun of him. 'Nae matter what ye try an dae for this toon,' he shouted back sadly, 'there's aye opposition.'

Sliddery Raa was a well-kept secret in the town, for it was down off a back lane behind Lang Raa, which was not only the main street, but the main visitor access from the outside world to the historic abbacy. Only the locals and the bowlers knew that to get to Sliddery Raa you had to go down Magill's Loanen between two derelict buildings on the Lang Raa, for it had neither street sign nor tarmac. A green wooden sign did have faded silver letters marking the entry as the way to the Bowling Club, but those in search of it would have to go right down to the bottom of what seemed like a cul-de-sac closed by a high privet hedge. Here was the hidden history, for behind the hedge was the much-photographed and postcarded Romanesque west door of the Abbacy, and Magill's Loanen must have been the original approach for centuries.

Montgomery Caldwell was treading this pad stiffly, like a man who knew where he was going but wasn't used to being up and about at half nine on a Monday morning. As he got to the hedge at the bottom of Magill's Loanen, he stopped to pull the clear wrapping off his packet of fags. He lit up as the cellophane floated down and blew under the hedge into the abbacy grounds. The wee shop at the other end of the Lang Raa didn't open on a Sunday, and it had been a long wait from Saturday night. 'Gumry,' as Montgomery was known for short, turned sharp right as he took his first deep drag and shook his match out. He surveyed the row of small garden gates along the right hand side of Sliddery Raa to see if anybody else was about at this ungodly hour. His own gate was the only one lying open, but he could see Sammy M'Clay out with the hedge clippers trimming the privet hedge opposite the club-house. It had to be kept low there so the evening bowlers would be able to see into the green from the club-house. 'Match on thenicht?' he shouted when he got as far as his own door. 'Na,' Sammy said without breaking the rhythm of his nibbling 'snip-snip.' Gumry changed his mind about going back in to his house. It was two years since his wife had left him, but he was still lonely and the M'Clay brothers were as near as he got to having some company. 'I never seen ye at the lodge,' he said, looking for some conversation point that would show him in a steadier light than Sammy. 'Na,' Sammy said, barely audible above the 'snip-snip.' 'Fag?' Gumry asked, offering Sammy a cigarette pulled out of his tight new packet. That did the trick, and the annoying noise pollution of the hedge-clippers was dealt with.

'Visitors,' said Sammy as a scraiching, through-other swarm of rooks rose from the tall trees that surrounded the abbacy.

'Bloody craas, they'd drive ye roon the bend.'

Sammy looked offended. 'The craas haes their uses,' he said, 'an ye micht fin yersel up there amang them someday.'

'Me? Dinnae be daft.'

Gumry barked a single scornful laugh. He knew they all called each other 'Kirkreeba Craas' as a sort of joke. You could enjoy that title as long as your grannie was buried in the grave-yard – as proof that you were born and bred here. But the idea that the 'crows' in the graveyard rookery were the souls of dead monks was an old wives tale.

History in Kirkreeba was local history, and religion was folk religion. Here what was truth and fact was too easily dismissed by the outside world as superstition.

'I don't believe in reincarnation,' he said after a superior-sounding pause. What he meant was, he didn't believe in 'freats'. After all, there were real monks buried there, and along with them real heroes of the Boyne and the siege of Derry, and real martyrs of the 1798 Turn-oot. And if you thought their spirits didn't hover over the place, then you didn't know Kirkreeba.

'C'mon ye eejit-ye,' Sammy said with a superior-looking smile, 'we'll take a wee danner up the toon til the visitors gan' hame.' The duties of a green-keeper, especially cutting the grass, were always suspended whenever day-trippers came to look round the ruins. No work-bell was needed when the trippers arrived or departed, for the crows sufficed.

Gumry and Sammy walked back up Magill's Loanen out onto the long bow-shaped street called the Lang Raa. The street was empty at that time of the morning, so they crossed the road without looking to the opposite side. From this corner, where Magill's Loanen carried on out of town like an arrow pointing to nowhere except up a steep brae to high-hedged fields, they could see the length of the Lang Raa. This was their usual stopping point.

'Ye don't think the monks were Buddhists, dae ye?' Gumry asked, not letting the subject go.

'Na, they were just like us.'

'Christians?' Gumry laughed as he asked if that was what Sammy meant.

Sammy laughed back, 'Na, ye gansh, they were just like us.'

Gumry dropped his cigarette butt on the footpad, leaving it to smoulder without beetling it into shreds with the sole of his shoe. His ex-wife Annie passed in his old car and Gumry turned his back on her the minute he recognised what used to be his. Sammy raised his hand, holding it up in a wave, and

Gumry tilted his head to give a mechanical half wave without looking to see who he was acknowledging. There was a silence as both men tried to think of what to say. 'Them monks had the life, hadn't they?' Gumry said eventually.

'Ay, just like the craas, not a care in the world.'

The corner boys of Kirkreeba often had the best of serious crack about the local stew of religion and history, but with a minimum of what a listener might call debate. It was all going on in their heads, all the same.

Gumry's mind was jumping back and forwards between two fundamental issues that were occupying his thoughts just then – the nature of the after-life, and the passed-by nature of his love-life.

'If them craas is all monks, then hoo come there's nests an scaldies an all?' he asked, making an unthinking assumption about their celibacy.

'There's a brave wheen mair craas than there is nests. Oniehoo, thon poem aboot the monks is the proof o it!'

'Thon oul poem Magill had? Sure that was just a load o oul nonsense.'

'Ay, the Lan' o Cokaygne, they caa'd it. The monks writ it themsels an it's aa aboot changin intae craas an fleein over tae watch the nuns swimmin naked doon the shore.'

'Och ay! C'mon Sammy, d'ye think I'm daft?'

'Did ye niver see it? How much d'ye bet? It's in black an white, oul Magill had it.'

'First I heared o it bein' ocht mair than an oul yarn. I'll believe it when I see it.'

The conversation ended, but not the deep thinking. Sammy was figuring out if Jeannie M'Clure might have kept a copy of the old poem after her father's death. Hugh Magill was never one to throw anything out, but his daughter had a fortnight of bonfires after he died. No wonder, when she learnt that some

American 'had fell intae the lot.'

Gumry was thinking back on his stupid fling with the same Jeannie. It was when he was doing some plastering work in their house. Nobody seemed to mind about that wee bit of fun until Jeannie's man, Jack M'Clure, tried it on one night at the bowling club with Gumry's wife, Annie. Jack, with too many gins inside him and not really capable of anything anyway, had assumed there might be some sort of a swap available. Temporarily offended, Jack spilled the beans about Gumry and Jeannie when he was told to catch himself on. Annie kicked Gumry out and relegated him to the monastic setting of Skiddery Raa. Then she found a man of her own.

Jack M'Clure had been President of the Kirkreeba Bowling Club for more years now than anybody cared to remember, and he had been part of the furniture in the club-house even longer. He was also the centre of the après-bowls scene at both sides of the bar with a commitment to his social duties that had debilitated him to the point where his wife Jeannie was often taken to be his daughter. Patron, key-holder, janitor, bar-rota organiser and principal customer, treasurer and stock-controller (for everything except the bowls and equipment which he left happily to Tam M'Clay) – these were the services he provided without a penny being paid to him, or for that matter, by him. Jeannie never had any aspirations to match her accidental status as the President's wife or the daughter of Councillor Hugh Magill. From her schooldays she had flirted with most of the men in the town, and still occasionally exercised her imagined rights of seniority just to prove she still had the pulling power.

'Tam, love, ye wudnae dae up my necklace at the back, wud ye? I cannae get the cleek in.'

It wasn't the first night that Jeannie had spent in Sliddery Raa, nor was it the first morning that Jack would wake up with his head in an ash-tray in the club-house next door. She gave a wee shudder as she felt the cold of Tam's fingernails against the back of her neck.

'Tam, yer han's freezing, love.'

'Is there oniewhere I could wairm it then?' Tam said with a greedy smile.

'I'll wairm yer backside for ye. Behave yerself. Look at the time.'

Jeannie M'Clure was as bitter as ever she was that Monday morning. The big house she was born and reared in was empty. It was where her father and all her forebears had lived and died in, and then her and Jack had come back to live there after her mother died. They had closed the big ground-floor room used as the Tea Room back then, for she had enough to do looking after her father, never mind having to contend with that. When the Solicitor wrote to tell her that the entire property was covenanted to some unknown American cousin, she was entitled to be bitter, and she told Jack so in no uncertain terms. 'Ay,' Jack said, 'it looks like that's all ye're entitled tae.' But there was her father's will: '… all contents and furnishings except fixtures and fittings considered part of the structure.' 'What's a fitting?' she asked Jack. 'Ocht that's screwed tae the wall,' he said. So everything went in a fury of bonfires and angry hand-outs. The 'reddin oot' of Hugh Magill's house and Tea Room was the talk of the town. Gumry had joked about it as the lads watched the process from their usual corner vantage point opposite: 'Jeannie was steamin' the wallpaper aff the waa's yesterday – 'are ye decoratin?' says me. 'Na, I'm flittin, says she.'

The whole insides of 'Jeannie's hoose' did go. Whatever wasn't needed for their new rented house at the other end of the Lang Raa was given away or burnt. 'Deil a stick o furniture thon Yank'll hae,' she swore, and true to her word, the bowling club got the tea-room tables and chairs for the club-house bar. The entire contents of Councillor Magill's library, shelves and all, went to the back committee room, along with a filing cabinet full of unsorted papers, a good solid dining-room table, half a dozen assorted easy chairs and twice that number of framed paintings and old maps and prints of the abbacy to hang on the walls. The historic setting of the green now had a club-house atmosphere to match.

Jeannie found her husband still in the club-house after another all-nighter. 'Quiz nane, hear nae lees,' was the M'Clure family motto. When Jeannie and Jack M'Clure were plodding back up Magill's Loanen on their way home to see what post had arrived and get a bite of breakfast, Sammy and Gumry were heading back down. The rooks had settled, and an unreal silence had returned to Skiddery Raa. Jeannie did a double take when she saw Sammy – til she realised it was Tam's twin in front of her and not the man she had just left behind.

Gumry was greeted with a warm smile, and that was all he got now from Jeannie since Annie had left him.

'Jeannie,' Sammy said, stopping in front of her, 'd'ye mind thon oul poem the monks writ aboot the abbacy an the craas an that?'

'I'm no' sure, what dae ye want it for?'

'Me an Gumry here's got a bet on, would ye still hae it?'

'It'll be doon in the filing cabinet in the club-hoose, if it's no burnt.'

Jeannie turned to go back down with the two of them and try and find it. She knew rightly it was there, in a blue folder, for her father had once raised her curiosity in the poem by telling her it wasn't suitable for a lass or a lady of any age to read. Jack was pulled two ways between going on home to get a proper lie down, or going back to the club-house with them. But when Jeannie started to talk about poems and stuff, he turned back again and said, 'Ach, I'll just away hame.'

'OK, see ye,' Sammy said, leading Jeannie quickly on down

the loanen to prove some point to Gumry about the abbacy and the Kirkreeba Craas.

The version of 'The Land of Cokaygne' that Hugh Magill had copied in his own hand was in a lined exercise book. It was *written in 1330 A.D.* according to a note that Hugh had added across the top of the front page. There were other bits and pieces in the blue folder, but at the top was a one-page typed letter from an American Professor that Hugh Magill had contacted thirty years ago, according to the date in the top right-hand corner.

'Ye need tae read the professor's letter first,' Jeannie said, 'for that's hoo my da fun' oot the poem was true.'

The jist of the letter was that this classic Middle English text 'with an undoubted Anglo-Irish provenance' was unlikely to have been written in the ancestral tongue of the original Kirkreeba monks, for it was in the wrong dialect of Middle English. The monks who came to the abbacy from the borderlands of what is now Scotland and England would have used a northern dialect, if not Older Scots. But the rest of the letter was positive, and explained why Hugh had kept it so carefully. A German scholar called Heuser had written the definitive study of the poem, and had suggested that from internal evidence it was written *about* Kirkreeba Abbacy, rather than *in* it. It was an attack on its worldly Cistercian ways by a Franciscan monk, possibly from Kildare. Southern or northern, Scotch or English, the archaic language of the poem had seemed strangely familiar to Hugh Magill, as it now did to Gumry and Sammy.

This rhyme was pure fantasy. It was about a gingerbread sort of abbey where incredible things happened of an 'indulgent' nature. The gripping thing about it was that it explained the origin of so many local folk stories and myths. Here were monks turning into birds, doing dirty things with the local lasses and nuns alike, and all the best scholars seemed to agree that Kirkreeba Abbacy was the very place the poem was poking fun at. Sammy and Jeannie already knew all that, but it was news to Gumry. If he ever needed proof of the local traditions about the Kirkreeba Craas, or the Nun's Well, or the medieval mystery of the 'Orange Tree', then here it was.

'Looks like they were on cocaine, right enough,' Gumry said as he waded through the make-believe lines about the '*mochil grei abbei*' of 'The Land of Cokayne.' He muttered about their 'heids being fu o sweetie mice,' with all this nonsense about the abbacy being built of food. But soon he was able to get more and more of the words by reading it out loud, helped by Jeannie's occasional prompting in his ear as she leant warmly over his shoulder.

> *Of white monkes and of grei*
> *Ther beth bowris and halles*
> *Al of pasteiss beth the walles,*
> *Of fleis, of fisse and rich met,*
> *The likfullest that man mai et.*
> *Fluren cakes beth the schingles alle*
> *Of cherche, cloister, boure and halle*

Even the cloisters where the bowling green was now had been given a special mention in the poem, along with an old and mysterious tree with exotic fruits, that made Gumry think of the rare herbs and other strange plants and trees that still grew in and around the abbacy. It also made him think of what particular tree Magill's Orange Tree Tea Room might have been called after.

But all of these blethers did little to satisfy Gumry's quest for knowledge about paradise or his curiosity about humans morphing into crows. Sammy saw he was losing the plot, so used his finger to bring Gumry straight to the lines that told how the young monks were better at flying with their sleeves and hoods opened out than any hawk or bird. When the abbot tried to get them down for evensong, they ignored him until he would take a young girl from the crowd and turn her white buttocks up and beat them like wee drums with his hand to call them down. When the monks saw that, they would fly down to the girl and gather round the lass so that they could all pat her bare white buttocks.

The yung monkes euch dai
Aftir met goth to plai.
Nis ther hauk no fule so swifte
Bettir fleing bi the lifte
Than the monkes heigh of mode,
With har sleuis and har hode.
Whan the abbot seeth ham flee,
That he holt for moch glee.
Ak natheless al ther amang,
He biddeth ham light to euesang.
The monkes lighteth noght adun
Ak furre fleeth in o randun.
Whan the abbot him iseeth
That is monkes fram him fleeth,
He taketh maiden of the route
And turnith vp hir white toute,
And betith the taburs with is hond
To make is monkes light to lond.
Whan is monkes that iseeth,
To the maid dun hi fleeth
And geth the wench al abute,
And thakketh al hir white toute.

The rhyme heated up further, as did its three readers, as it went on to describe a nunnery that was nearby, alongside a river of sweet milk where the young nuns go out in a boat and strip off for a swim. Out fly the young monks to the naked nuns, where they swoop down and take one each back to the muckle grey abbey, and teach the nuns a prayer with their legs up in the air. Not surprisingly, Gumry read these lines a lot more carefully as Jeannie pressed against him.

> *An-other abbei is ther-bi,*
> *For-soth a gret fair nunnerie,*
> *Vp a river of swet milke,*
> *Whar is plene gret of silk.*
> *Whan the somer is dai is hote,*
> *The yung nunnes takith a bote*
> *And doth ham forth in that riuer,*
> *Both with oris and with stere.*
> *Whan hi beth fur fram the abbei,*
> *Hi makith ham nakid forto plai,*
> *And lepith dune in-to the brimme*
> *And doth ham sleilich forto swimme.*
> *The yung monketh that hi seeth,*
> *Hi doth ham vp and forth he fleeth*
> *And commith to the nunnes anon,*
> *And euch monke him taketh on*
> *And snellich berith forth har prei*
> *To the mochil grei abbei,*
> *And techith the nunnes an oreisun*
> *With iambleue vp and dun.*
> *The monke that wol be stalun gode*
> *And kan sey a-right is hode,*
> *He schal hab, with-oute danger,*
> *Twelve wiues euche yere …*

Gumry was a bit shocked at the mixture of religion and soft porn. Twelve wives a year for the monks was a bit much, to say the least. The poem had even ended with the 'Amen' that was sometimes still used in the lodge-room – *'so mote hit be.'*

It didn't help Gumry's disturbed feeling when they went back outside to look at the carved stone gargoyles up high along the outside walls of the ruined abbacy. Sammy pointed out the first and third ones from the back which were definitely women's faces. And the second one along was, as sure as sin, a naked stone backside squatting out over a blocked window opening. 'An then there's the Nun's Well, isn't there?'

'Ay,' thought Gumry with the dismay of a child that had just discovered that Santa doesn't exist. His mind went from thoughts of the garden of paradise to the Nun's Well that had always been at the back of Sliddery Raa. That was where the lay brothers' dormitories used to be. Why was there a well there at all, when the burn had been culverted from the start to run right through the monastery? And why was it dug just there where the fantasy fruit tree was supposed to have been? The lay brothers of the old abbey would have known, but the M'Clay brothers wouldn't be interested.

'Some boys them monks,' Gumry said, trying not to be seen to take it all too seriously, 'and they were hardly guid-leevin. Eh?'

'Na,' said Sammy, 'I keep tellin ye. They're just the same as us.' Gumry was quiet. He was thinking. The last thing he wanted was a dozen wives, or even a fancy woman. Getting back the one he had in the first place would be nice. One thing was for certain, he wasn't going to be chasing after Jeannie anymore, nor be building any nests with her. He watched from the open door of his house as Sammy went back to his 'clip-clip' at the hedge and Jeannie walked slowly back up to the Lang Raa. Her head was down and she had the gait of a burdened soul as she retraced her husband's steps towards home.

When Jeannie got to the Lang Raa, she turned right instead of left, past the deserted Orange Tree Tea Room and fading paintwork of her old family home. Her head was still down as she avoided looking in the windows. She pressed on as the street swung round towards the visitor entrance of the abbacy. The minute she opened the side gate attached to the east end of the ruins and stepped into the old burying ground, scores of rooks skailed in all directions from the surrounding trees up into the sky. The wails of the 'Kirkreeba craas' were deafening, but only lasted a few seconds as Jeannie made her way over to the Magill family burial plot under the open gothic tracery of the abbacy nave's east window. Her head was still bowed as she read the fresh lettering put up for her father. Enough space left for herself, she thought, unless the American had been left this part of the estate as well. Her eyes slowly worked their way up the stone, half registering the ascending ancestral record.

Perched nervously on top of the next headstone she spotted a solitary black rook, shuffling with its wings twitching as if getting ready to fly off. For a split second – that stayed with Jeannie for a long time – their eyes met. The cold, stone-like stare from the bird couldn't have been more different to that of Jeannie's. Her eyes filled. As it flew off to join the others, Jeannie touched its point of departure on the top of the headstone and gave a single, sobbing gulp.

Chapter 3

Back to Monday Morning

Kay was glad to see David leave the bookstore to get his breakfast coffee. The concept of the working breakfast was something she never associated with her husband. But she liked to get him out to tidy up the bookwork and accounts before the customers arrived. And this morning Pat Mahood would be dropping off the unsold books from the Faith Bookstall. It was a sort of focus for the folk who came to the weekend coffee mornings at Crossroads, so the number of books sold didn't really matter. Kay loved the Saturday morning fellowship events with children, friends and friendliness everywhere. The place was buzzing with purpose-driven lives, in stark contrast to her own home. It seemed that everywhere else, even at the Crossroads, coffee and books went together. Everywhere that is, except in their bookstore. Why on earth was David so opposed to the idea of expanding the bookstore in that way? He just couldn't be bothered with change. Kay had so many things she wanted to do and David hadn't an interest in any of them. There seemed to be nothing going on in his life while Pat and the others at church were so positive about everything. Pat was the best and most energetic pastor in the town, and he wasn't even full-time. He was also the best teacher at the High School, although he consistently rejected all offers of full-time posts and promotion there too. It was best to get David out of the way before Pat came, for his usual manner in front of all her friends was curt, bordering on the rude, and Pat wouldn't be used to that sort of thing from adults.

It wasn't just church fellowship occasions that Kay didn't mind when David made himself scarce. She liked her own time first thing in the morning, so it suited them both for David to walk into the bookstore and open up by himself. Her daily devotion routine and her prayer diary were things Kay took seriously, but in private. Prayer triangles were O.K., but not prayer partners, for they were too personal. She had no wish to bring up the question of David's shallow, empty life in front of others, apart from with her Maker.

With David and his stubborn resistance to the basic tasks packed off to the coffee shop, the book-keeping backlog was sorted out and tidied away before Pat was due. Kay tidied the uneven books on the shelves, and then tidied her hair. In the looking glass she replaced her reading glasses carefully on top of her head, like a tiara. She sometimes imagined herself as a pastor's wife, but not in an unfaithful sense. She never harboured thoughts like that. No, or at least very, very rarely. 'Love is a decision, not a feeling, honey,' she often said to David by way of assurance, and she liked to practise what she preached. Her heart jumped slightly when the door opened and sounded an old store bell that David had bought in Monterey to add antiquarian atmosphere.

'Oh Pat, don't carry all those in by youself,' Kay said, coming out from the behind her corner desk to relieve him of the load, 'any more in the trunk?'

'No, that's the lot. Is David about? I want to ask him something.'

'He's down at Steinbeck's, but he should be back soon. Why don't you come in and wait?'

Pat hesitated, 'Maybe I …'

'I wanted to talk to you myself about getting some help for the meeting next week.'

'Sorry, I'm not going to be there. But I need your help. Could you hold the fort for me?'

'Of course,' Kay said instinctively with a forced smile to hide the scunner his changed plans had caused her. 'I'd love to,' she lied.

'In fact, that's what I need to talk to David about.'

'What, you mean for David to help out too?'

'Oh no, sure he's no interest in our church mornings. I meant to … well, I'd better speak to him first.'

Just then the door opened and Kay's heart sank further as she saw her husband come through the door to the double jingle of the store-bell. David stopped in his tracks when he saw Pat, and then his wife's expression. 'What's he sniffing about in here for?' he thought.

'David. The very one I'm looking for.'

The next thing that came into David's mind was triggered by guilt. Was the man that had sold him the box of books known to Pat, and was he here to try and get the valuable first edition back and accuse him of dishonest dealing?

'Me?' he said, 'what's up?'

'Anna King, you know, works in the coffee shop?'

David hesitated, pretending to be unsure who he was talking about, and not look guilty a second time. 'Who is this guy?' he began to think, 'does he know what's going on in my head, or is it obvious I find even her name bewitching?'

'Joseph King's daughter,' Pat prompted.

'Oh, yeah. What about her?'

Pat glanced at Kay as he explained it was something he need- ed to talk about in private. David looked carefully at Kay as she forced another smile and said, 'Of course, I'll just …' and disappeared into the back. She was hurt, and David noticed, but he thought that Kay had been reading his mind too.

Pat Mahood's Garden Gate project was the most important thing in his life, more so than his church, although that was because of his view of God and not in spite of it. The project was out of sight from Orange Grove's squeaky-clean centre – down among the old fruit loading platforms at the railroad sheds. Pat had got use of them for next to nothing, for they were empty since Weston's new Fruit Packing and Storage Depot was built in Main Street. The new depot, despite its fancy facade, had a sordid back end with steel roller shutters facing the poor district and trailer park behind the railroad tracks. Nobody wanted to see the business end of the district's industry right in the middle of polite down-town. And nobody wanted to see the poor folk who lived and sometimes worked in that place. All that end of things was deliberately pushed out of sight so that it could be out of mind, and so it was with Pat's project among the down and outs. Kay wouldn't talk about it, other than as another example of the sort of thing that proved how good a man Pat was. And Pat didn't talk about it much either, not as if it was his project anyhow, although he thought of little else even when he was at his paid work.

David and Kay saw Pat Mahood as a pastor. Anna and Joel King thought of him as a teacher, for they had both done English Literature in his class at the High school. But George Hamilton at the coffee shop and everybody else involved at the Garden Gate saw him as the foreman in the workshop, the warden of the sleeping quarters, and the kitchen and canteen manager rolled into one. The residents, however temporary, also knew him in a more personal way. If this had been a monastery, Pat would have been their father confessor, life-tutor and friend. In fact it was very like a monastery, without the trappings, and they certainly had the poverty, but without the vows.

George Hamilton was generous with his left-over food from the coffee shop. He got Anna to take it down to the Garden Gate at a slack time each day, and allowed her extra time to call at the food-store to pick up the frozen foods that had just gone past their sell-by date. It all had to be taken quickly to Pat's big double freezer in the Garden Gate kitchen where the residents risked some of the best cuisine in town. But things seemed to be going missing. Strange, for Anna helped out in her own time at the Gate whenever her father would let her, and could have all she wanted anyway for the asking. And on top of that, George had noticed that the money and food orders in the coffee shop didn't always tally. He had a quiet word with Pat who said he thought he knew what was going on. 'But don't go firing Anna,' he told George, 'I promise you she can be trusted.'

When Pat brought the subject up with Kay's husband, David, he told him the bare minimum. If this was dishonest of him, so be it. He wasn't going to tell him about his biggest worry of all – that Anna was being treated badly, or worse, at home. Certainly she was frightened to go back at night, and he had noticed the same when she was still at school. Her brother Joel was different, but disturbed as well. No other teacher wanted him in their class, and the feeling was aggressively mutual. But Pat saw a glimmer of interest in books and fantasy comics. Joel was a loner, and sometimes came into Pat's empty class room at break-times to take a book down off the shelves and flick through it. At first it was an excuse, and he only pretended to read. Then Pat gave him things to read he thought he might like. 'There's a man in this story reminds me of the way I think you are going to be when you get older,' he said once. 'Good or bad?' Joel's interest was rising. 'Well, that would give it away, wouldn't it? See if you can spot him for yourself.' That was the first proper book Joel read properly. And it was the first time he tried to see himself as others did. 'It's not what you think you are, you are. It's what you think, – *you are*,' Pat told him with a smile when he revealed the character he had in mind and Joel had said, 'Never!' But since Joel got fired from his first job in the Weston's Fruit Depot for pilfering, he had avoided all contact with Pat. Whatever Pat suspected about Joel's visits to the coffee shop while Anna was working, it wasn't in line with his real hopes for the boy, and he wasn't going to tell that to David either.

'David,' Pat said, still holding him by the elbow where he had led him to the front of the bookstore, 'I have a big favour to ask of you. It's not for me, but for Anna King and her brother.'

David was immediately happy to help if it meant Anna thinking well of him. 'If I can,' he said. 'What is it?'

Pat motioned for him to wait while he picked up a Steinbeck Heritage Trail fold-out map and leaflet from a pile at the bookstore's cash register. 'You helped George Hamilton put this together.'

'Sort of,' David said cautiously. 'I know his books are banned at your school, but …'

'By the school,' Pat said with a disapproving shake of his head, 'not by me.' David thought of the High School's edict of 'dubious moral content' on *East of Eden*, and decided to leave that debate for another day. Pat would have liked to discuss his own unorthodox views on the content as well, but not today. 'Look,' he said, anxious to get to the point. 'I really like this leaflet. And I was going to ask you if you would help bring on, sort-of sponsor, Anna's brother Joel as a Trail guide?'

David had thought that the Heritage Trail guided tours of Orange Grove and District were part of George Hamilton's business, or at least the town's Chamber of Commerce. But it now transpired that it was, somewhat secretively, run by the Garden Gate project. At least that explained why delinquents like Joel King were involved.

'Joel King? Is he not a bit …?'

'He's got a better taste for literature than any youngster his age I've had at school for ten years. And he knows the area like the back of his hand.'

'Well …' David was uncertain. 'Does he want to do it?'

'I haven't asked him yet. In fact, that's the other thing I wanted to ask of you. I can't get speaking to him for his father, but I thought if you asked Anna about it – without mentioning me or the Garden Gate – then their father would be happy enough. He thinks everybody at the Gate is a do-gooder or a no-good.'

David was about to ask why George Hamilton couldn't speak to Anna, seeing she worked for him at the coffee shop, and if George didn't actually run the Tours, they certainly started off from his place. As the leaflets said: *'Tours depart Wednesday – Saturday, from Steinbeck's Coffee Shop, Main Street, Orange Grove at 10.30 a.m.'* Of course, George was some sort of distant cousin of John Steinbeck's, on his mother's side, and he had a guaranteed coffee-shop trade on those mornings of the tours. But then Magill's Bookshop was on the tour too, and he had been happy to sponsor the leaflets. Of course he would be happy to speak to Anna, and would do that as soon as he could. It was a long time since he had felt so good about helping someone out. What a day! He heart gave a little lift when he remembered his first edition find. It gave him another thrill when he thought of the news about Uncle Hugh's place in Ireland, and he was still feeling thrilled when he thought of his mission to speak to Anna.

Chapter 4

As the Crow Flies

In a straight line, the distance from the well at Joel King's house outside Orange Grove to the Nun's Well at Kirkreeba is almost exactly 6000 miles. Of course, going round the world actually isn't travelling in a straight line, unless you dug straight through. Not a single family in Orange Grove could be traced back more than six or seven generations without the lines taking them straight back to Europe, Asia or some other continent. Not a single one of the ancestors of the early settlers with Scotch-Irish connections had set out from their ethnic nests with the slightest notion of ending up in Orange Grove. David Magill's family was the nearest thing to an exception, but only because he had come to nearby Orange County with his father and mother forty years back. And he was the only one with a serious interest in tracing his roots – an interest that was revitalised with the news of his Kirkreeba inheritance.

'Do you remember our honeymoon in Europe, Kay?' David asked his wife, without an ounce of romance on his mind.

'Of course, honey, how could I forget?'

'Do we still have that notebook you kept, with the gravestone inscriptions at Uncle Hugh's?'

Kay's interest in the conversation would normally have plunged at that point but the news of David's inheritance had re-kindled her passion for his family tree. When they were just married, David was happy to leave all that stuff to Kay. He was more than happy, for he took it then as a sign of their 'one-ness' and of Kay's total integration into the Magill clan. But now he wasn't so sure. It was more like controlling him again by being better informed about his family than he was himself. 'I guess so,' he said when Kay found the notes. They confirmed that David's grandfather and Uncle Hugh's father had been brothers, so their father, Robert Hugh Magill of Easterton, was recorded in Kirkreeba Old Graveyard as the common link. *'Died 12ᵗʰ Feby. 1861, aged 79 years,'* the notebook said, with Kay's note in brackets underneath that he must have been born 1782.

The more Kay warmed up to the subject, the more David's interest cooled. 'That made,' said Kay, 'Robert Hugh the earliest Magill in the Magill family plot, unless there had been older stones or older burials.' The only other clue she had was from an old memorial plaque in flaky sandstone on an inside wall of the abbacy ruins. They had taken a photo of it at the time, but all that could be made out was was a coat of arms with three birds on a shield for the 'Reverend David Magill,' Minister of this and the neighbouring parishes 'obiit 15 Octobris 1633.' David pointedly reminded Kay that Uncle Hugh had said that this David Magill was the first of their connection to 'come over fae Scotland.' They weren't sure at the time that it wasn't just a touch of blarney, but the solicitor's letter had the best possible proof. The will was based on the same reverend gentleman's legal insistence on an eldest-male line of inheritance.

'A gap of a hundred and fifty years, from 1633 to 1781, should be easy filled in, seeing they lived in Kirkreeba all the time,' David said finally, as if that was the matter closed for the time being.

Kay's enthusiasm for a possible move had taken David by surprise. With all her commitments in Orange Grove, and her family connections, and her ownership of the bookstore, not to mention not having Scotch or Irish roots, David had assumed it was out of the question for her. He thought that it might be an excuse for going off on his own with a clear conscience. He even fantasised about going off with Anna.

But Kay was not to be underestimated. She would love to try running a tea-room or coffee-shop, rather than a book-store. People and hospitality, rather than dusty old books, were more her cup of tea, literally. It was David who began to see the downside of moving back to a country he had stopped calling 'home' forty years back. 'It'll drive you mad,' he said, 'the folk aren't the same as us you know.' 'Of course, honey, but tourists love heritage trails and history the world over – you know that better than anybody, don't you?' 'I guess so,' David said with a hint of resignation in his voice. But he wasn't to be underestimated either, and he began to formulate a plan for tourism links between the Orange Tree Garden Gate project and the Orange Tree Tea Room in Kirkreeba.

'That's a fantastic idea,' Kay said to David's surprise, 'I think it was meant to be, and we could theme the tea-room with orange-tree plantation murals on the inside walls, and tubs outside with little orange trees growing. It would be just like a home from home.'

'But orange trees don't grow at home.' David realised he had called the old country home, and that he quite liked the idea.

'Well honey, we can get artificial ones then, can't we?'

'Maybe the tea-room wasn't called after our sort of orange trees, if orange trees don't grow there.'

'Now you're just being silly,' Kay said, but she thought better of asking him what other reason there might be for the name. David was going to explain why he wasn't just being silly, but he thought better of going into it as well. He imagined how out of place the likes of Anna or Joel King would be in Kirkreeba. 'The folks at home aren't the same as us you know,' he said.

• • • • • • • • • •

Pat Mahood and David Magill were sitting discreetly at the back-most corner of the coffee-shop, as a rag-taggle assembly of eight or nine folks, including two children, gathered for the Steinbeck Heritage Tour of Historic Orange Grove. Anxious not to lose any strays or customers for his coffee-shop, George Hamilton was out as usual with a welcoming smile and a business-like clap and rub of his hands.

'You guys all stopped by for the tour?' he said as he made a back and forward sweep with his arms out and hands up-turned. 'Take your time, we've a couple of minutes yet.' After a two-second pause, he added, 'Yep' in answer to a threesome who hadn't asked any question, 'you've time for a quick coffee.'

It was to be Joel King's first unaccompanied run as a tour guide, and he sat by himself at one of the front tables, alone, nervous and strangely out of place in his home town. His sister Anna was nervous too, not sure whether to acknowledge her brother, serve the waiting group, or stay watching in the background with Pat and David.

'Right folks! Everybody here?' George declared the start of the tour by gathering the scatter into a group with a circular pulling motion of his hands. Pointing in equally dramatic fashion to Joel, he said, 'And here's your guide for today. Now you're all in good hands, for nobody knows the town better. But I'll let Joel introduce himself.' Joel raised himself slowly out of his seat and came forward. He looked uncomfortable and his back-stage supporters held their breath in case he dried up. 'Hi,' he said loudly and confidently as if a switch had been thrown, 'my name's Joel King and I'm gonna take you round some pretty cool places. Now, has anybody been round the town before?'

'No? Good.'

The group was easy enough to please, for they wanted to have a good day. There was a young couple, only interested in being together and doing something together, if the whisperings in each other's ears and perpetual smiles were anything to go by. There were two older, well-dressed women with silk headscarves and casual bags big enough for cameras, notebooks and anything else that might be needed. They seemed to be together, but another man about the same age seemed to be on his own at times and then known to them at other times. Then there was a family with youngish father and mother and two children, the oldest being a sullen and bored looking boy of about fourteen or whatever age it is that boys start wanting to look as if they are not with their parents. The girl was a perfectly-behaved seven-year-old.

'Y'all from California?' Joel asked, seeing that the young boy just didn't want to be there and had asked in a loud voice 'I wanna go back?' There were some nods and some shakes of the head in answer to Joel's question. 'Who's from farthest away?' he said, looking straight at the boy. 'Ohio,' shouted a voice from the back. 'Anybody beat Ohio?'

'New York,' said the boy enthusiastically, sensing a win and keen to announce he was better than the rest.

'New York! The Big Apple! Well, that's the furthest ever.' The boy was smiling and proud. 'Did you know that John Steinbeck lived in New York too when he wrote *East of Eden*, even though the book was all about these parts?' The boy didn't know the book never mind the author, but Joel had got his attention. Looking away, Joel asked, 'and can anybody else think of another connection between the big Apple and the original Garden of Eden?' 'Yip,' shouted the boy, 'There was a big apple tree in the Garden of Eden.' 'Sure, that's right. Hey, I think I'm gonna need your help today. Will you stick beside me?' The boy was delighted to be a tour guide assistant.

It almost didn't matter to the group if Joel didn't know anything of substance, he was a nice young man that seemed to like them. He was a natural. David was taken aback in a nice sort of way, for until today he hadn't found him to be anything more than a shy and servile boy – someone who said 'sir' after every question and answer. 'Well done, David,' Pat whispered to his fellow adjudicator, and Anna almost burst with pride as Joel ran through the programme as he was handing out the Heritage Trail maps. The group were smiling back at him.

'Before we head off, this is Mr George Hamilton,' Joel said pointing out George with both hands in imitation of the man he was introducing. 'Mr. Hamilton is the proprietor of this coffee-shop, which isn't 'Starbucks' spelt wrong, but – what is it called?' he asked, turning to his assistant. 'Steinbecks,' the young New Yorker said, doubly pleased to have passed his first test.

'That's right. Believe it or not, Mr. Hamilton is related to the same Hamilton family as John Steinbeck's mother and grandfather. And the very Hamilton family that the *East of Eden* story was based on in real life. But we'll see more of that when we get to the gravestones at the First Presbyterian church – and after we go to the old fruit-packing depot where the workers were locked out in the depression'.

Pat, George, David and Anna watched as the group disappeared round the corner of Weston's into Main Street.

'Oh, thank you, thank you Mr. Magill. Wasn't he great?' said Anna holding her clasped hands tightly with excitement into her breasts.

'He sure was honey,' David answered, sharing her excitement in intimate detail in his mind. He wanted to hug her, but conscious of the company, said, 'Don't thank me, it was Pat here.'

'Oh yes, thank you too Mr. Mahood. More coffee?'

'Yes, Anna. Give them whatever they want. It's on me this morning,' George joined in the general celebration.

As David made his way back to the bookstore to be ready for Joel's group at the end of their tour, he found himself once more thinking of Anna. He imagined her life outside the coffee-shop, doing things at home, doing ordinary things at the shopping mall and going for quiet walks. What a spell she had on him. No matter what her interests were, they would be intriguing. And, if Joel was anything to go by, what hidden depths! Despite the difference in years, she wasn't the sort of girl to be like others of her age. Those looks and those smiles, she definitely thought of him as something special too.

Pat Mahood turned down the offer of yet more coffee, cookies or muffins. 'No George, but, got a minute?' he said, pulling out an empty chair beside him.

'Sure, what is it?'

'I wanted to ask your advice about setting up a small business by myself.'

George was sure he wasn't about to be asked for financial help. That wasn't Pat's way. 'I'm not much of a businessman, Pat. And there's no end of stress. I wouldn't recommend it to any body with a secure job like a teacher, or a pastor.'

'Well, that's the point,' said Pat, 'I haven't any desire to become self-employed. But I am thinking of giving up my job at the High School.'

'What on earth for? You're one of the best teachers, and when you see the way the likes of Anna and Joel have turned out, surely it gives you a great feeling.'

'Yeah, but – well look at Joel today. You've no idea how many good students I've seen leave school and do nothing. The Garden Gate Project is where my heart is. And look at Anna, I've never seen her as happy as when she's here working for you.' Pat was going to add, 'apart from Sundays at Crossroads,' but instead he said, 'I would even put the Gate before being a pastor.'

'Is that not a contradiction?' George asked.

Pat thought silently for a minute. 'You're right, he said. I wouldn't put it before my pastoring. But I would put it before my *job* as a pastor.'

Before George could offer any particular advice, Pat said, 'Thanks, George. That really did help. You've given me the answer to my question.'

There was a stunned silence at the meeting of the church elders at Crossroads.

'I have been thinking about this for weeks now,' Pat said as he told then of his intention to resign as their Pastor.

Kay was not alone in feeling let down. 'I don't understand,' she said. 'Are you having a crisis of faith?'

'No,' smiled Pat, 'I should have said I've been praying about it for weeks now.'

'Are you taking up a full-time job at the school?' 'Are you leaving us to go to another church?' The questions on people's lips were legion. The questions that were also on their minds, but unspoken included, 'Have you had a breakdown?', 'Do you need counselling?'

'Please,' Kay said, 'don't do anything final till you've had a word with David.' It was a desperate move, but the best she could think of to give them time to find a way of keeping him. Pat looked in silence at Kay. 'Guess that wouldn't do any harm,' he said, knowing full well it wouldn't do any good either.

It seemed as if Pat and David were becoming regular customers as a twosome at Steinbeck's. But there was no high-pressure sell coming from either quarter at this meeting. David had no intention of keeping his promise to Kay that he would use his best endeavours to talk him into staying. 'We are having great run of book sales at the store on tour mornings. Joel must be stimulating their interest.' They both smiled contentedly. 'And he's even buying some books himself – I feel guilty about charging him.'

'Joel's a great guy,' Pat agreed.

'This Garden Gate centre of yours – what is it all about?'

The pastor in Pat knew that this was a classic 'permission

evangelism' moment. But he kept the focus on Joel. 'Why don't you ask Anna or Joel? It's the folk down there that it is for.'

'You mean getting them set up with a job and stuff?'

'Not really, it's not about giving them what we think they need. Sometimes it's even a refuge from that sort of pressure – or worse.' Pat paused for a minute as if he was trying to think of a way of explaining. 'Joel,' he continued, 'I think sometimes he has a better handle on it than me.'

'Is the Garden Gate name connected to the Garden of Eden? I sort of assumed that, like the *East of Eden* thing.'

'I don't think it looks much like the gates of paradise,' Pat smiled as he thought of the pearly image. 'Joel was telling me how the tour groups always ask that question.'

'And what does he tell them?'

'He goes into the Garden of Eden story, and the two trees in the middle.'

'Two? I thought there was just the Tree of Knowledge.'

'Yeah, and I guess you thought the forbidden fruit was an apple too. But Joel tells them that the gate to the east was guarded to close off the other one, the Tree of Life.'

'That's a bit too deep for me,' David said, retreating rapidly. But it was too late. His question about the Garden Gate was answered.

· · · · · · · · · · ·

Anna King had a secret she hid from her father. It began as a little thing, and suddenly it became a terrible secret she hid from all around her. When she first saw Will there was only a cardboard box between them. He had called at Steinbeck's on a delivery run from Weston's to pick up some surplus bits and pieces for the kitchen down at the Garden Gate. Anna had brought the box out the back to the truck, and saw the back of his checked shirt and blonde-tipped brown hair at the nape of his neck just before he turned. Then his bare forearms touched hers as he took the box from her and he hesitated as they made eye contact. His arms were golden brown with a warm furry down of sun-bleached hairs, unlike Anna's which were browny-brown and satin smooth. Anna held on to the box without thinking. In fact, she was thinking, but it was of an embrace or, more innocently, a dance. His greeny-blue eyes were smiling kindly. The pupils of her brown eyes were fully dilated and an open book.

'Are you Joel's sister?' he asked as they both held on to each other through the box. Anna nodded. At that time Joel was still working in Weston's.

'I'm Anna and I help out down at the Gate after work,' she said.

'I could give you a lift down. Would George let you out to show me where these go?'

'Oh no,' Anna said in a tone that meant and wished the opposite.

It was not until their next encounter at the Gate that Anna learnt Will's name. He was a Canadian, from north of Vancouver, and working his way down the West Coast in no particular hurry. 'Mexico is as far as I want to go, but maybe this is far enough.' Anna thought how much she could offer him if he really meant that. Her little secret was her fairly obvious heart-burning crush on Will. But as things developed, Anna worried about her father finding out why she was spending more and more time helping out after work at the Gate.

When Joel got fired from Weston's, George Hamilton noticed that the pilfering and discrepancies at the coffee-shop had suddenly stopped too. But Pat had told him not to jump to conclusions – and not to blame Anna either. As far as George was concerned, that only left outside people with access to the kitchen, like Will Dawson. Again Pat told him not to blame Anna on that either.

'Who's this guy Will Dawson?' Joseph King asked Joel as they sat at their roadside fruit stall in front of the house. The apples were everywhere now as the fall was just beginning. It was cool enough to sit outside the shade; a fact appreciated by hens and tethered dogs as well. Joseph had heard the name mentioned when Joel tried to explain to his father how he had got fired from Weston's for something he didn't do.

'Just one of the truck drivers,' he said. 'He's not from these parts.'

'I didn't think so,' Joseph said. The name had stuck in Joseph's mind, not from anything Joel said, but from Anna's sharp head-turn when she heard Will mentioned.

'He's not one of them churchy folk of Pat Mahood's is he?'

Joel laughed. 'I hardly think so.'

There is no telling what all Will Dawson helped himself to in Orange Grove before he suddenly disappeared. Eventually, Pat asked about him at Weston's to try and confirm Anna's conviction that Will had just gone on a quick trip to Mexico. They had talked plenty about her mother's home town over the border, and she knew that he would soon be back.

'Sorry, Anna,' Pat said once he knew the truth, 'looks like Will has gone back up north to Canada.'

'He can't have,' Anna said, 'why would he?'

'His visa. And it seems he works back there every ski season.'

Pat alone knew what a devastating effect this news was going to have on Anna. Her faith in human nature, and love itself, would be shattered. But what Pat didn't know was that Anna's little secret had become a terrible one. The only pleasure she had sought with Will was the purest thrill of real and trusting love. There was no lust whatsoever, so how could she be pregnant? That wasn't what was meant to be. She just couldn't understand it and much less could she tell any body about it. Would the folks at Crossroads understand? She didn't even dare ask herself the same question about her father at home. As for Pat, well he seemed to be able to read her mind. The one good thing was that he had left his jobs at the school and Crossroads. There was no reason why her old school friends, or the folks at Crossroads, would know.

When David learnt Anna's secret, it hit him like a bombshell. 'Can't you see for yourself?' Pat said when David asked him at the coffee shop why Anna was off sick for another morning. Pat's morning run to Anna's father's place for fresh eggs had become one of the most challenging tasks of his fraught-filled day. 'There's no fool like an old fool,' David thought when the implications sunk home. It wasn't so much that his fantasies about Anna having special feelings for him were exploded. But it had never even occurred to him that she might have had any other love interest, never mind a boyfriend – and never mind that! If he couldn't have faith in his dreams, what else was there?

Kay Magill was mentally prepared for a new life in the old world. Orange Grove was no longer the place of her dreams. So many people had let her down – and none more so than Pat Mahood. The idea of starting afresh in Kirkreeba was the only exciting challenge on the horizon. David? He sometimes gave her the pip, for he behaved as if the whole world revolved around him. 'The more I warm to the idea of the Orange Tree Tea Room,' Kay thought, 'the cooler David seems to be on a move.' He was such a stubborn man, and so set in his ways it would take a bomb to move him.

Chapter 5

Bringing It All Back Home

'Take care with the passports, honey,' Kay said to David as they were unpacking at their new home, 'put them somewhere safe.' That was easier said than done, thought David, for in their newly-named, new home of Orange Tree House, there was hardly a stick of furniture.

They had started looking round auctions and second-hand furniture shops for bits and pieces that would fit in with the big old property, for David's inheritance had been stripped to the walls by his second cousin Jeannie. What Kay thought was in character was very different from the real period style, and from what the local expectation was too. The 3-piece suite she had picked was about forty years old, and would have been cheap when it was new. The side-boards, cabinets, tables and chairs were all old-fashioned rather than old, and a weird mix of styles. Nothing would have passed muster as an antique, but David had no interest. He just let Kay get on with it.

David Magill opened his passport absent-mindedly and looked at his photograph. It always gave him a shock to see himself at the age he actually was. He looked like a grumpy old man. Not like himself at all. His hair was grey in overall tone, as was his moustache. Yes, he did have some grey strands, but he was able to screen them out with selective vision when he looked in the mirror. He stretched his chin up and felt underneath to prove he didn't really have all that loose skin and scrawny bits. And where was the twinkle in his eye that Anna had often returned? David then opened Kay's passport and examined her photograph. It was the other way about. It must be an old one, for she looked younger and prettier, like she used too when they were first married. He had forgotten that she once was attractive.

'Which of these colours do you like best?' Kay asked, holding the underside of two paint-tin lids in front of David.

'Where for?'

'The kitchen, of course, where do you think I've been working all morning? I like this here, but the undercoat would do either one.'

'I don't know,' David said in a way that meant, 'I couldn't care less.'

'It's all right, honey, I'll do it, but I just want to know you're happy with it.'

'Look. I haven't time for picking colours and things like that,' he snapped back. Kay had noticed that David seemed to be 'down' all the time now and, particularly since they had decided to move to Kirkreeba, he was often irritable too. 'A bit of a middle-age crisis,' she thought and decided to give him a squeeze. When that didn't produce the smile and response she needed, Kay gave him a peck on the cheek and went back to painting the kitchen with the creamy colour that she had already decided on.

The old, empty Tea Room was the last to receive Kay's interior design attention, but not because she had lowered it from top of her list of priorities. It was going to need major renovations before that part of the vision could be realised, maybe even structural work. The inside walls of the main front room had cracks in the plaster. Part of the back corner of the ceiling had fallen down. The back rooms that were connected into the rest of the house had already been fixed up in Uncle Hugh's time, but all traces of a kitchen had been removed. Kay had to completely revise her vision from the picture that she had developed in Orange Grove. The space was bigger than the bookstore, but the layout was completely different. She stood in the middle of the tea-room deep in thought, trying to imagine how the elements she wanted would fit in. The walls would need re-plastered anyway before a themed mural in terra-cotta shades could be painted. At least there was room for a dozen 4-seater tables with bent-wood chairs and green and white checked tablecloths. Depending on the customers, they might develop a more up-market linen and table-silver finish, but for the time being, a bohemian look would be best. One thing that was completely out was the idea of outside tables on the sidewalk, as was the norm back home. The 'fitpad' in front of them in the Lang Raa was barely wide enough for two people to pass. Even if it had been the width of the road, it would be brave folk that would sit out there sipping tea through the sort of weather and ridicule that Kirkreeba could throw at them.

From the outside, from the viewpoint opposite where the M'Clay twins and several other Kirkreeba Craas had their traditional perch, the old Tea Room was on the right-hand, ground-floor corner. The 'Orange Tree' wooden facia board over the old shop windows and door had long had its name painted out in the same colours as the rest of the house, and there was a small window on the gable onto Magill's Loanen. At the back there were blocked-up openings in the stone yard wall, including a door that might provide public access to the back yard. But Magill's Loanen was not, at the minute, a grand enough avenue for the concept of tables out the back to be developed.

'First things first,' thought Kay, as she tackled the problem of the crumbling plaster inside the Tea Room. She had asked in the local shop down at the far end of the Lang Raa if there were any builders about. 'Plenty,' she was told, 'in next door.' But next door meant the pub, the Duke o' Montrose, and she hadn't had the pleasure of exploring its delights yet.

'Do not,' said David, 'spend any money on builders without speaking to Peter Close the solicitor first.' Kay was quite happy to spend her own money on this part of the project. She didn't quite understand the concept of the perpetual estate which meant that they only truly owned the value of any improvements – and that meant keeping a record of all money spent. However David did understand that bit of the deal only too well. On a rare burst of initiative he got the details himself from Peter Close. The last improvement and repair work done during Hugh Magill's life was the re-plastering of two rooms on the ground floor only five years back. The paperwork was signed by Hugh Magill's daughter and the work had been carried out by Montgomery Caldwell, 5 Skiddery Raa, Kirkreeba.

'The boss in?' Gumry said when Kay opened the door to him. Fortunately for Montgomery Caldwell, Kay could hardly understand a word he said.

'A hae wrocht here afore, ye know, roon the back,' he explained to David who was only a fraction the wiser.

'Pardon?'

'A've work't here before, roon the back,' Gumry repeated.

'Oh, are you the plasterer? Mr Montgomery? Come in.'

'Magumery's my Christian name,' he said, following David as Kay led them into the Tea Room. 'Ye for fixin it up then, Mr Magill?'

'I would like to,' Kay answered, 'but I think we need all the walls patched first.'

'It's aa boased. She needs scutched aff an done fresh – it's oul lime plaister wi horse hair. Like A fun oot the back when A done it for Jeannie M'Clure.'

'How much do you think that would cost?' Kay asked nervously.

'Oh, we'll not faa oot over it. A'll gie ye a price an drop it in themorra.'

Although Kay hadn't understood much of what Gumry said, it didn't show. She just waited smiling as Gumry was talking, and then carried on with what she wanted to say. David guessed as much for he was well used to much the same treatment.

'Thon boy'll sort ye oot aa richt,' he said to Kay when Gumry had left. Kay was not amused.

'Stop that! There's no need for you to talk like that as well,' she snapped. The stress of it all was beginning to take its toll. She suspected that Gumry had been laying it on thick and talking far 'mair braid' than he usually would, just to put her in her place as a blow-in.

'You'll have to get used to it if you want to get the tea room opened, never mind talk to the customers,' David said. He was somewhat chastened, but smiled to himself anyway.

Gumry was standing on the other side of the Lang Raa with a couple of other cronies the morning after he had delivered his building work quotation. Strictly speaking, 'standing' might be a misleading description, for Gumry was lounging at an angle of 80 degrees against the corner of a row of two-storey houses where Magill's Top Loanen carried on out of town. One of the M'Clay twins was sitting on a window sill. The houses were old, and although stone-built, the only visible stone through the rough unpainted 'harling' dash was the broken, stepped line of the row's window sills. The door surrounds were obviously cut stone too, but these were all covered with gloss paint. 'If stones could speak, the houses opposite could tell a story,' David thought as he spotted Gumry and his friends from his own window. In a sense the stones could speak, for the door-surrounds each had a deep, smooth, mouth-sized missing chunk on the right-hand side. These notches were all about chest height, and whatever made them belonged to the mists of history, at a time before they were painted over. The Kirkreeba Craas resting on these stone houses, if they cared to speak, could tell a surprising lot in their own way too. Sammy M'Clay, for one, remembered his mother telling him how the folks in the Lang Raa used to come out and stand at their front doors every Sunday to sharpen their carving knives on the sandstone door jamb. They wanted to show their neighbours they were eating beef, and they all sharpened their knives in this Sabbath ritual display – whether they really were having meat for dinner or not.

Of all the stones in Kirkreeba, none could speak like the head-stones in the old graveyard against the east of the Abbacy, for that was the whole purpose of their inscriptions. When David paid the place his first visit since his honeymoon, he went alone and took his own notebook. The unpainted, rusty iron-gate that was the only way into the burying ground squeaked noisily as he went through it, but there was hardly any other noise, even from the rooks. On either side of the gate were two strong stone pillars built of the local bluestone, with a carved sandstone plaque which declared an ominous welcome: 'Enter not *Ye Dead* save by *The Gate* of *True Life* and Knowledge.' Tam M'Clay was cutting grass at the back, and David recognised him as one of Gumry's friends. Tam ignored him until he saw that he had gone straight to the Magill Family Burial Plot under the east window of the Abbacy.

'You the new man in Jeannie M'Clure's hoose?' Tam asked in a way that demanded more than one answer. David nodded, not really wanting to address the fact that he hadn't seen or spoken to his second cousin yet. 'Where is her new house?' he asked pretending an interest. 'Her an Jack M'Clure's leevin in a new bungalow in Westerton oot the Ballywester Road. But they're doon Sliddery Raa behin ye maist o the time.'

David waited til Tam wandered off before pulling out his notebook. He noticed the new inscription to Hugh Magill at the bottom of the Robert John Magill head-stone, and a bowl of fresh flowers in front of it. The top of the stone was a single round arch like most of the others in the graveyard. Unlike the others which had carved decorations of stylised plants leaves, geometric flowers, rosettes and whorls, several of the Magill ones had a full spreading tree. In no particular order, David jotted down people's names and dates and townlands. He put the notebook back in his pocket and walked over to where Tam was raking his long grass cuttings up into a pile.

'How come the Magills have spelt their names different ways?' David asked, having noted that there were Magills, McGills, MacGills and even a Magilton.

Tam shrugged his shoulders. 'They cudnae spell, A doot.'

'But Magilton?'

'Ach, thon was way back when some o them thocht get the name o the hale toonlan' o Easterton changed tae Magill's Town.' Tam laughed at the thought.

'What about the Orange Tree Tea Room?' David asked, re-alising how their idea of 'Orange Tree House' would reflect on Kay and himself as being a bit pretentious.

'What about it?'

'How did it get its name?'

Tam shrugged his shoulders again. That was not a subject for discussion with strangers. 'Jeannie's the yin for the history,' he said, 'ask her.' He paused and then added, 'or gang doon tae the bowls an see the oul maps an things her man Jack has pit up.'

As Tam started to gather up his tools to leave, David followed him back to the graveyard gate. The whole town seemed to be built of the same local bluestone that formed the bulk of the Abbacy itself, and the graveyard was surrounded by a high wall of the same material. 'The old gate pillars here,' he said, 'they must be some age.' It was a comment rather than a question, so it didn't elicit any response from Tam. 'What's the story behind that?' he asked, pointing sideways at the 'Enter Ye Dead' plaque with his thumb.' Never mind the Abbacy, every stone in the place seemed to have a story to tell.

Tam ignored the plaque, for writing could speak for itself. 'These pillars here were jist pit up in the echteen hunderds. Echteen an sixty tae be exact.'

'How do you know that?' David was impressed, and he was even more so when Tam pointed out that the top three quarters of the pillars were built differently from the older bits below.

'The new bit's in better coorses, but it's quarry stane an the rest is aa field stanes.' Indeed, although the 'new' stonework was geologically the same, it was all sharp, broken corners in contrast to the smooth rounded stones that must have been brought up by horse-drawn ploughs and collected from the fields.

'Eighteen-sixty?' David asked. There had to be a bit more to it than 'reading' the stonework itself.

'Ah, that was the big fecht here that led to the end o the Church of Ireland as the Established Church, wi the tithes an all that.'

David's expression of disbelief was the only question Tam needed. He continued with the explanation. In 1860 a local rector of the Parish church had tried to stop a Presbyterian funeral from using the graveyard. It was Church property and he hadn't been asked for permission. So, when the coffin-led procession was coming along the Lang Raa, he locked the old gate and disappeared to the Rectory. His intention was just to wait for the minister to come and ask permission. 'Well,' Tam said, 'naebody turned up, for the boys had just got some horses an chains an pu'ed the hale gate doon, pillars an all. Wi yin thing an another, the magistrates was called in, there was a big coort case, an the outcome o it all was the Presbyterians were in the richt an the hale Church o' Ireland had tae be disestablished.'

David had no doubt that parts of the story were true, but he was only concerned with one historical story – the history of his own house and the Orange Tree Tea Room.

'What are ye yerself?' Tam asked David directly. The question took David aback.

'You mean, what church do we belong to?'

'Ay.'

'Well, I don't really, but I suppose we're Presbyterians.'

'That'll be a first for the Magills,' Tam answered. He broke into a knowing smile. 'There'll be another fecht when they come tae plant you in the Magill plot.'

That, however, was a subject David definitely didn't want to talk about.

Jeannie M'Clure was down at the bowling club as well as her husband Jack the night that David and Kay dropped in as Gumry's guests for a drink. Kay was tee-totally nervous about the occasion, for she didn't know exactly what compromises of her standards were expected. But she felt the need to cultivate a good relationship with Gumry as her trusted advisor with the renovations. David was just in for a nosey, but had in mind Tam's comment in the graveyard about old maps and things on the walls. He had spotted a coloured picture-map of Kirkreeba dated 1625 – 'surely that has to be a copy, or it would be worth a fortune,' he thought. But he couldn't get studying it right then, with all the crowds in for a night's socialising.

The regulars, the whole 'social membership' of the bowling club were watching the new inhabitants of Magill's house carefully, weighing them up. David and Kay were aware of that and tried to act naturally. They were not sitting alone, for they were guests of Gumry, who seemed very popular with everybody wanting to show that they knew him. Gumry didn't just sign them in and leave them to it, but sat with them as Kay talked loudly and proudly in a Californian accent. But David was aware of being watched in a slightly more intense way by one of them. She was an attractive girl a bit younger than him, and they kept making eye contact which in itself aroused David's interest. 'Who is that sitting with the man that works in the graveyard?' he asked the man behind the bar as he was getting another drink for himself. 'That's the wife, Jeannie,' Jack answered without a hint of embarrassment, for David had all the signs of being about to make an approach. 'Your cousin,' Jack added with double effect.

Immediately, David went over to Jeannie and introduced himself. 'Come over and join us, and meet Kay,' he said. Jeannie seemed reluctant, but obligated. They chatted for a while, not as a foursome, but with Kay engaged in gaining mastery over Gumry, and David engaged in exploring the mystery of this long-lost cousin. Kay was not impolite, however, and showed a genuine, if fleeting, interest in this daughter of Hugh Magill. Jeannie would have a memory of the Tea Room when it was in full swing before her mother died. But it would be indelicate to bring that up straight away.

'You must come round for dinner some evening?' The invite was not particularly welcome.

'We'll see,' Jeannie said. She could see that Kay was more interested in Gumry. 'I'll maybe just land in on you some time.' As she said that, she laid her hand on David's forearm for a lingering second. David looked instinctively at his wife who was laughing loudly at everything Gumry said. He might as well not have been there. Jeannie seemed offended in some way and stood up to go.

'You off?' Kay said.

'Ay, I'm off.' Jeannie went back to the table where the M'Clay twins were without even looking at Kay.

David was left with a very uncomfortable feeling. Had he said something to annoy Jeannie? There was something about her that intrigued him. She was quite attractive, in a haunting, soon-to-be obsessive, kind of way. And she seemed to be intrigued by David too, maybe even found him attractive, or so he thought. 'I hope Jeannie didn't think we were being offhand,' he said to Kay.

Gumry looked at the pair of them and said, 'Weel, yous are moved intae the hoose she was born an raired in, an she hasnae got over her father yet. He's no' a year deid ye know. Gie her a bit o time an she'll be aa richt.'

David was to return to the clubhouse regularly in the next few weeks. Partly it was to check out the old maps and things, and partly it was to talk to Gumry and find out more about how Jeannie was. And partly it was in case Jeannie might be about.

The 1625 map of Kirkreeba was under glass in a picture frame on a side wall of the committee room. Jack told David he could take it down and put it on a table. 'Ye can get it copied sometime, if ye want,' he said, 'Jeannie wouldn't mind, for it's really hers anyway.'

'Oh, I wouldn't do that without asking,' David said, taking off his glasses and using one lens as a magnifying glass.

The '*Plat of the toune of Kerkreeba*' was drawn by the appropriately-named '*Thos. Raven, Surveyor,*' and was a beautifully-coloured birds-eye view of the village. The *Abbacie* was shown as a mostly roofless but complete ruin, complete in the sense that it was round all four sides of the cloister. A few isolated cabins were strung along a curved outer line that must be where the Lang Raa now was, and Magill's Loanen was shown as the main road leading to the Abbacy with the annotation at the far end '*Ye Road to Westerhouse, Westerkirk and Schottelande.*' Among all these details, there were a few that caught David's attention most of all. Outside the Abbacy on the far side to 'Easterhill,' was a marshy creek that nearly reached the West door of the Abbacy Church and ended at '*Sliddery Forde,*' and not far off was a paddock marked '*Ye Ball Greene.*' But the most exciting discovery was a larger-than-the-rest tower house on the site of David's own house. Apart from an even larger castle outside the town belonging to '*Wm. Edmondstone, Gent.*,' the only other dwelling with its owner identified was this one, '*Mr. Mackgill.*'

David had begun his quest for knowledge of his own origins by discovering, from Tam M'Clay, that maybe the 'stanes could talk' after all. His quest then was only about his own Magill family, starting with the Rev. David McGill as the first of them to arrive from Scotland. But now he had discovered that the stones on a building could perhaps speak clearly about the buildings they were part of. And now he was just as intrigued by the history of his house as he was about his family. He needed an interpreter of this newly-discovered language, or a teacher. Jeannie M'Clure was the obvious answer to all these needs. She had all the right qualifications.

Chapter 6

Heart of Stone

'A never seen stour like it,' Gumry said as he emerged choking after stripping the old plaster off the walls inside the Orange Tree Tea Room.

Kay put a handkerchief over her mouth to investigate before the dust settled.

'I hope the walls are safe,' she said, 'what about that crack?'

'Thon's no' a crack, it's an oul blocked up wundae. Look at the oak timber lintel. A fun' yin just like it, roon the back, when A was workin for Jeannie.'

'David would be interested in that before it gets covered up again.'

David was interested, but Gumry had to point out to him that the blocked windows were on the wall between the tearoom and the rest of the house. 'So that means this pairt o the hoose is ouler than the rest.'

Kay had more faith in Gumry's expertise as a house detective than in her husband's. 'How old do you think the house is then?'

Gumry was flattered that Kay asked, and took, his advice about all sorts of things. That showed she was actually quite a nice person, he thought.

'As she stand's, A'd say aboot twa hunner year. Georgian, like.' He didn't feel the need to explain that the bit they were standing in could be as old again.

Before Gumry could plaster over the blocked-up window opening, David had a poke round for himself. There was a part of the opening that was filled with red bricks, and among them was a small fist-sized hole with a round piece of thick glass in among the loose lime mortar. He tried to hoak it out with a screwdriver, but it didn't want to come.

The next day Gumry got it by taking some of the surrounding bricks out, after Kay had told him David wasn't able to. It was a long, green-blue glass bottle with a rolled up piece of paper inside.

'Gie that tae the boss,' Gumry said, proudly holding the intact bottle out to her, 'there's a bit o paper in it.'

'Oh, do you think you could you get it out for me? I don't think David could without breaking the bottle.'

Gumry looked round him for something that would fit through the neck of the bottle.

'Bring it into the kitchen and I'll get you a long skewer. Would you like a coffee?'

The note in a bottle was something left by the builders at the time the walls were last re-plastered. As it turned out, that was 1868 when the room was being altered to make it into a tea-room. It read,

THE ORANGE TREE, KIRKREEBA

These Premises
were repaird and a new front added thereto
by Robert Hugh Magill for his son James.
The men engaged were –

> *Samuel Girvan, Mason*
> *Hugh Lavery, Mason*
> *Saml. Montgomery, Carpenter*
> *Jas. Caldwell, Plasterer.*
> *William N. Girvan, Painter.*

Written by   *William N. Girvan Sept. 1868*
Witness   *McIntyre Girvan.*

Kay couldn't have been more excited about this discovery if it had been buried treasure. She had it mounted in an old glass-fronted picture frame and hanging on the wall before David even came home. But first of all her eyes had caught the name 'Jas. Caldwell' as Gumry opened the document out on the kitchen table and held it flat. 'Is that one of your relatives?' she asked Gumry.

'Ay, it is. But so is aa the rest. We're aa the yin soo's pigs roon here, ye know.'

'The history is so alive, and everything here is so old,' Kay said, staring intently at Gumry's muscular shoulders under his tight checked shirt, as he leant forward with his elbows on the table. She had a remarkable ability to be saying one thing and be thinking something completely different at the same time. Gumry was more straight-forward. If he had been more hard-hearted, he would have begun to flirt with this fresh blood from the other side of the world. But all he felt was a relaxed and comfortable friendship swelling up. He smiled warmly as their eyes made prolonged contact.

The next weekend, Kay left David in the house reading a book as she walked down to the shops at the bottom end of the Lang Raa. Across the street from her front door, at their usual Saturday morning watching post, were Gumry and Sammy. 'Hi Gumry,' Kay called over, waving over with a broad grin to them both. To Sammy's surprise, Gumry ran across the street to Kay as if she was an old friend, and pointed back at the front eave near the high roof of her house.

'Wait an A'll show ye something,' he said. 'Ye can see it from here. The near end o the hoose is rinnin in a different line fae the rest. D'ye see?'

'I think so.'

'That shows ye. The hale thing was built in twa bits. Like A was telling ye aboot the blocked-up wundaes. The Tea Room end is far ouler than the rest.'

David and Kay had both come to the same conclusion about the Orange Tree Tea Room being older than the house – rather than being an addition the other way about – for different reasons. Kay saw the proof in the building itself and the way in which its stones spoke. In simple terms she trusted and believed Gumry. David saw the proof in the written record of maps, documents, inscriptions and books, particularly those he had recently been shown by Jack and Jeannie M'Clure down at the bowling club. In simple terms he was developing one of those hopeless and destructive crushes on Jeannie.

'It's all worked out fine in the end,' Jack M'Clure said to Jeannie as he ran his finger round the inside of his stiff white shirt collar and adjusted his bright, obliquely-striped tie.

'Like what?' Jeannie asked in a tone that disagreed wholeheartedly.

Jack continued to preen himself in front of the bedroom mirror, oblivious as always to the fact that his wife did not agree with him on all matters of substance. His wavy, receding hair was combed and slicked straight back and he was now using the comb to fluff out his distinguished, greying sideburns.

'All this,' he said waving his comb vaguely round the tidy new bungalow and towards the perfectly manicured front garden. 'Our own place, and not having to live in your parents' house.' He might have also mentioned the benefits of being the Bowling Club President's wife, but instead added, 'and the Magills want tae join the Bowling Club as social members. They're just the sort of professional fowk we need tae raise the tone, aren't they?'

Without waiting for a response, which wasn't coming anyway, Jack went through to the breakfast room for his morning routine. These rituals were just what he thought were becoming to a man of leisure, like someone in his position. First, he collected the morning paper from the front hall. This in itself was a mark of distinction, for usually the morning papers were only delivered in the town. Then he passed through the kitchen and selected a wine bottle from the rack of dark green and brown bottle ends. This arrangement disguised the fact that the bottles were all screw-tops of cut-price vintage. A large plunge of dark red something was slopped into a big glass, and Jack settled himself where he could supervise 'his gardener' at work over the top of the sports page.

Sammy M'Clay spent about half an hour a day trimming and weeding in the garden of 'Green Acre.' He rode his bike from the Lang Raa out the Ballywester Road every morning about eight o'clock with Jack's paper under his oxter. The garden was well short of an acre, but Jack argued, 'not when you add in the bowling green.' Sammy's duties as green-keeper were liberally and flexibly interpreted. Of course, the one thing Jack wouldn't have was Sammy's twin brother, Tam, round at Green Acre on 'relief' duties. His home was his castle, and whatever Jeannie did elsewhere was her business, as long as it was elsewhere. While her husband was making his morning appearance on the Presidential balcony, Jeannie's mind, as always, was elsewhere. Some mornings Jeannie's body was elsewhere as well.

'The Bowlers' Service is in the Parish Church the year,' Jack said. 'Mr M'Intyre wants us tae do the readins, so he does.'

'Read away yerself,' Jeannie said, 'I'll no' be goin near it.'

'The Rector'll be disappointed.'

'An what's wrang wi that?'

Jack looked at her as if she had just arrived on his planet. 'You'll be lettin doon the club an all.'

Jeannie responded with an ever-growing feeling of alienation by using a single word. 'Guid!'

Jack was a wee bit shocked, for he thought his wife was happy with the way she could do whatever she wanted now she didn't have a crumbling old house and a grumbling old father to look after. He assumed a lot. The real problem was that he didn't think outside his own world at all.

'Maybe Kay Magill will?'

'Will what?'

'Do yin o the readins, what d'ye think?'

Jack had touched a raw nerve. 'She goes tae the Meetin Hoose,' Jeannie objected, 'anyhow, dae whatever ye want.'

It would have been the last straw for Jeannie if Kay's 'churchyness' had been inflicted on Kirkreeba Parish Church, instead of the Presbyterians. Then she thought, 'no, the last straw would have been if David Magill had been inclined that way.' Imagine if he was to walk into office on the Select Vestry in the Parish Church, or even worse as Church Warden like her father. Not that Jeannie darkened her church door anymore. The last time she spoke to the Rector – and as far as she was concerned it would stay the last time – was just after her father died.

Mr M'Intyre had used the word 'taken' when he talked about her father's death, as he often did in those situations. 'No!' she had screamed at him and all that he stood for. Her mother was 'taken' from her when she was only a child. That hurt them all, but then that dreaded Bailiff returned with a vengeance last year. He 'took' not only her father, but her home, and – just because she was a woman – her rightful inheritance. That wasn't just possessions, but a whole sense of worth and belonging. She looked at her semi-detached husband as he patrolled his detached bungalow, slapping his folded newspaper against his thigh as he walked. 'Holy Matrimony' had a lot to answer for too. It had taken her self-respect along with her surname when Jack M'Clure turned out to be Jack M'Clure. Just look at him! The bottle and his petty social ambitions had taken him in spirit too. At least those demons couldn't be blamed on God, but everything else could. And the church was part of this Magill curse. At the heart of all these compound losses she was suffering was the Reverend David McGill's damned legacy of 1633. It was a perpetual curse dressed up as an earthly blessing.

Now, to cap it all for Jeannie, this new David Magill was not content with all he had taken possession of, but was drooling at the mouth every time he saw her. Had he not taken enough of hers? She knew that hungry look only too well, with his mind's eye peeling off her clothes. In her bitterness, she had her own fantasies. Revenge would be sweeter still if she found David attractive, but she found his neediness had the opposite effect. But the ultimate prize would be to take back possession of the whole lot by producing the next Magill heir herself. 'Not,' she thought at the edge of reason and fantasy, 'beyond the bounds of possibility if David was man enough for it.'

Jeannie knew she had things David was after. She knew the full history of the Magills and the Orange Tree, but she was damned if she was going to part with that cheaply. She knew the full effect of her boulder-shaped cleavage too, especially compared to Kay's pebble-dashed frontage. That was another thing David wasn't going to get his hands on in a cheap way either. Although her life was full of regrets, she had no sense of guilt about her open life-style as far as the other men were concerned. Apart from one, maybe. That short, fumbling session with Gumry back in her old house, did nothing for either of them. Jeannie did feel guilty still about Annie Caldwell and what it did to her, for neither her nor Gumry thought it was worth shaking a leg at. But neither of them wanted any more of that from each other anyway. 'Unless,' Jeannie thought, 'he's back in there doing the same for Kay Magill.' In that case, she might have to make another move.

Gumry Caldwell had not got over the end of his marriage, and he wasn't going to make the same mistake again. He had plenty of male company, and enough male bonding to last him a lifetime, as Secretary of the Kirkreeba Lodge. But that wasn't enough. He had got used to the special female companionship that his marriage to Annie had provided. If there was anything he missed, that was it. Kay might be a perfect replacement for that in some ways, but not as far as going the whole hog was concerned. A slight compensation for his loneliness was the crack at the Lodge, especially on the well-attended nights when he could see how many of the brethren came just to get away from the wives. Gumry threw himself more and more into the Order, sometimes even travelling up to the city for classes of instruction for degree and lecture work. Being Secretary involved far more work than being in the Chair, for he had to do all the correspondence and keep the Master right as well. But he kept an interested eye on the other activities, most of all getting the new banner ready for its unfurling.

The 'new' banner for the Kirkreeba Lodge wasn't really a new banner, but the old one with a face-lift on one of its sides. Bro. Tam M'Clay was in charge, for he was handy with a paintbrush and, as it turned out, a natural artist when it came to murals and that sort of thing. The old picture in the inset had been a scene from the 'Battle of Athlone, 1691,' and it was being replaced by a large likeness of 'The Late W. Bro. Hugh Magill, J.P.,' which Tam was copying from a photo Jeannie had given him. Not everybody was happy about the change of subject matter, but it was hard for Gumry to object without sounding disrespectful or offending Jeannie – especially in the circumstances.

The photo of Jeannie's father was the best she could find, and it was a painful experience sorting through the albums to pick it. There were a few taken of him on the Twelfth wearing his old faded sash, but he was lounging in the Field in a pose totally unsuitable for parading through the length and breadth of the county. Then she found a studio portrait with gold writing across the bottom 'Jas. Abernethy Photographer.' It was just the right one for it made him look like a statesman, but she had to lend Tam the sash as well so he could superimpose it. Now it was nearly finished, Jeannie had been given a preview to make sure she was happy with the likeness before the official unfurling and dedication service. Jeannie was invited to the ceremony, even to say a few words, but declined when she learnt that the Rector was doing the dedication. 'Na,' she said, 'it'll be eneuch for me tae see my da wi his chest puffed oot again, comin doon the Raa on the Twelfth morning.'

Gumry had more problems unfurling in his life than the new banner. He felt that Tam's affair with Jeannie was getting dangerous now they were beginning to like each other in a friendship sort of way too. Maybe it was jealousy, not about the physical relations but the friendship thing. The only woman on the horizon that might offer him the same soul-partnership feeling, without the carnal knowledge, was Kay Magill. This uncoupled thing was the big hole in his life, but it was a need he had to keep to himself among his mates for fear of being thought less of as a man. And maybe the two sides of marriage couldn't be uncoupled anyway.

'What church do you go to, or maybe you never go?' Kay asked Gumry in the middle of a conversation about whether the wooden floor of the tea-room should be lifted before or after the stripped and scudded walls would be plastered. The question took Gumry by surprise for she had broken several social conventions in one go, in the way only an American could get away with. She knew she had never seen him at the Presbyterian Church, and that didn't leave too many other options. He fumbled for a non-committed answer. 'Now an again,' he said.

Kay was unsatisfied with the religious life of the new community she had adopted. The only religious opinion she shared with most was the conviction that Sundays were dead in Kirkreeba. She was prone to making deals with God in return for his help with her own plans to extend his kingdom. A fellowship house-church was what the place needed to escape from its denominational prison. In fact, the tea-room might become the first meeting-place outside of good 'front' rooms. Gumry might even become her first convert outside of the town's gospel-greedy. Kay saw no contradiction in having a 'house church' in a tea-room, and she was dissatisfied with such nit-picking among the religious people in her new environment. They were riddled with an alien cultural baggage she had no time for. She wanted a sect that was non-sectarian, for even the deeply committed Christians were bogged down in petty traditions that she neither understood nor cared about. Paul Whitely of First Kirkreeba Presbyterian Church was different, for he had been trained as a minister in Carolina, but he was the only one with that broader vision. Kay believed that she and Paul were probably the only proper Christians in the town, but she had some reservations about Paul too.

'What do you think of the Rev. Whitely?' she asked Gumry.

'He seems aa right.' The only time Gumry had heard him preach was at the Bowlers' Service last year when it was his turn among the local clergy, apart of course from a few dozen funerals. 'The Rev. M'Intyre's a guid man tae.'

'I can't say I've met him. Is he Bible-based?'

'Oh ay,' Gumry said, thinking of the obligations Mr. M'Intyre had undertaken as Chaplin of the Lodge. But that was something he wouldn't have dreamt of mentioning anyway. There wasn't going to be much meeting of minds between Kay and himself on the subject of religion. If Kay realised that half the men she knew as neighbours made up the core membership of Kirkreeba's 'Invincible Heroes', she would have been horrified. Gumry could sense that she wasn't exactly keen on his brand of religion, so for Kay alone, the Invincibles would remain a secret society. That 'out-of-sight, out-of-mind' feeling would change when she would see them all parading behind Hugh Magill's banner next Twelfth – with him at the heart of it.

Just after Kay and David had first arrived from America with all their baggage, they had seen the Invincibles on parade behind their old banner. David had come to the front door to watch, for he hadn't seen that sort of thing since he was a child. Kay watched through the window in curiosity at first, hardening into disapproval, as if it was an alien invasion of some sort. Neither of them had any idea of who the individual folk in the Lodge were, even though the reverse wasn't true for Gumry and all the rest, trying not to gawk at the new arrivals.

The next Twelfth might be a revelation for Kay, but it was more than likely she would have other plans for the day. For the time being, there was real scope for her special friendship with Gumry to grow. Kay was determined to put her faith into practice and meet Gumry at his point of need. First of all, she had to help him see more clearly what his needs really were.

Chapter 7

If Looks Could Kill

David Magill had always been a dreamer, but as he got older he was turning more and more into himself with his growing obsessions and fantasies. Kay was excluded from some of these for obvious reasons of marital harmony, but as far as his open desire to exhume the living details of an ancestor who had lived 400 years ago was concerned, Kay just let him get on with it. She had long been used to him having his head buried in a book. Now with so much real work to be done, he had his head buried in the sands of time as well.

The wooden floor of the tea-room was taken up by two or three men Gumry had brought in, now that Kay had put him in charge of the whole operation. David was interested in their progress, as long as each new bit of work revealed more. It was a bit like turning another page of his book. This interest would evaporate when the plastering and covering-up stage got started, and then the book would be closed again. Today's exciting new chapter was the discovery under the wooden floor of an older, stone-flagged floor. It had enormous worn slates the size of the head-stones in the graveyard. When this was added to the blocked-up windows, and an enormous blocked kitchen hearth, there could be no doubt about the age and importance of the tea-room end of their house. Whenever David looked at the work in progress, he became fixated with the historical investigation. His other obsessions were not pushed out of sight however, for Jeannie was the one who could best help him unravel all this.

When Kay looked at the work in progress, she had to focus forwards on the future instead of back – on the tea-room vision. The orange-tree theme would need a Mediterranean or a Californian touch.

'How long will it take for the walls to dry out before we can paint them?' she asked Gumry long before they were ready for the new coats of plaster.

'Aboot three or four weeks, wi the amoont o stuff that'll need pit on the walls – tae cover the reuch, like.'

Gumry and his helpers kept their 'stuff' out the back of the Magill house, in one of the outbuildings off the yard. They sat out there for their tea-break too, despite Kay's repeated invitations to come into the kitchen. As they sat inside an old stone cart-shed with a large double door, Gumry noticed that the long timber beam over the door opening on the inside was an ancient re-used oak beam. It was another discovery, for it had all the clues that proved it was the original massive breast beam from an old kitchen hearth in a castle or the like. On the top side were notches for the upright oak staves of a chimney hood canopy, and along the front bottom edge was a carefully-shaved decorative chamfer. When Gumry showed it to David, and then pointed out the matching cut-off end of the beam that was embedded in the front stonework of the tea-room about head height, David's mind was working overtime. He was filing this new piece of information, and for a brief moment, he was impressed with Gumry and said so in a patronising sort of way.

The oldest man in Kirkreeba was Dan Lockhart. He had lived in Sliddery Raa for every single one of his 96 years but now he only emerged for an increasingly rare shuffle up and down Magill's Loanen. Dan had been out with the 'Invincibles' last Twelfth in a fancy, horse-drawn carriage, sporting his new 80-year, long-service medal. But that was an exception nowadays. David wouldn't have known anything about that, but he had spotted him once out on the Lang Raa, and wondered who this pale old man with a long black coat and white bushy eyebrows could be. He was stopping every six or seven steps to lean on his stick and look around him. When he stopped he seemed to be talking to himself. As David walked up behind him on his way to the shop, he was struck by how like a crow he was. If he had known about the Kirkreeba Craas he might have thought Dan was in some sort of transitional phase, and would soon, finally, just fly away.

'Hello,' David said loudly and politely to Dan, turning to smile as he passed him. Dan stopped in mid-shuffle and looked sharply at David without any sign of a response. As David walked on he could feel those sunken, bird-like eyes piercing into his back.

Although David was still reasonably fit and healthy, in body if not in mind, he was now having difficulty sleeping at night. Often he would get up in the middle of the night and wander round the house. In those ramblings his mind could only shuffle through the things that were bothering him. When he found that he was talking to himself, he came back to earth with a bump, but before long he would fly away once again on some other flight of fancy. In the wee small hours, with everybody else sleeping, those were the times he could sit alone downstairs in his dressing-gown. With no distractions he could imagine what the house was like when the Rev. David McGill lived there in the 1620s. He almost daren't go into the tea-room for fear the bare stones of the floor and walls really did begin to speak, literally. He wasn't sure about believing in life after death, but definitely not in any earthly after-life in the form of ghosts or that sort of thing. Well, not in the cold light of day anyway.

In his nocturnal ramblings, more often than dreaming about the clerical patriarch of his Magill clan, David's mind would return to Jeannie. He could imagine what the house was like when she lived there as a pretty young thing. And just as easily, he could picture her as she looked now, looking after Uncle Hugh when he had gone 'away with the fairies.' It was a short step from that to less realistic, but more exciting, fantasies about Jeannie living back in the Orange Tree with him, now.

Jeannie M'Clure, thought Kay Magill, had just about the hardest heart of any female she had met in her new list of acquaintances at the bowling club. She was utterly wrong in that, as she was in her growing conviction that the same Jeannie had designs on her husband. In that respect at least, Kay and David had something in common, for David had no idea that his obsession with Jeannie wasn't reciprocated in the slightest way.

Kay spoke to Jeannie during one of her visits to the clubhouse down 'Magill's Avenue', (as she called the Loanen). She didn't go there as often as David, for all he seemed to be interested in doing was poring over the Magill family archive that Jeannie had deposited down there. Kay's occasional visits were motivated by an instinct that she needed to keep a discreet check on Jeannie, to make sure it was her books and not Jeannie herself that David was pawing over.

'I was wondering,' Kay said to Jeannie on one of these occasions, 'if you knew anybody who could paint?'

'Pictures or walls?' Jeannie said in a sarcastic tone.

'Both, sort of. It's for the renovations we're doing to the tearoom. I would like a frieze of orange-tree foliage painted round the inside, or maybe even a mural or something like that. We had a lovely one of the orange trees in a plantation back home in Orange Grove.'

Jeannie smiled. 'I know the very person,' she said, 'Tam M'Clay. He's very talented in all sorts of ways, and, believe it or not, he has painted a brave few murals.'

'That's very kind of you,' Kay said, 'we're not at that stage yet, but if you wouldn't mind asking him for us?'

'My pleasure,' Jeannie said with as nice a smile as Kay had ever been given from that quarter.

When David checked his bedside clock, it was 4.16 am. He always went down the stairs in the dark so as not to disturb Kay. The kitchen was warm, but the living room was chilly, too cold to sit down and read, even if he could have concentrated. It was one of those occasions when all sorts of things were racing through his head. David paced the kitchen trying to make two conflicting ideas gel. In Jeannie's books he had discovered a host of information about Rev. David McGill. The same gentleman was a man of substance, whose father was also called David McGill and had been Lord Advocate to King James VI of Scotland. Both father and son shared King James's obsession with witchcraft and the devil, or so it seemed. The records had shown that they both associated themselves closely with their monarch's writings on demonology in the 1590s. But after that, the Rev. McGill took nothing whatsoever to do with King James's Bible translation project of 1611, even introducing the Geneva Bible into Kirkreeba Parish Church about 1630. That was a bit of a mystery, for the Rev. David was obviously at the vanguard of King James's other divine mission to plant the promised land of Ulster.

Now that sort of mixture of history and religion was of interest to David. And when he thought that this man was his own direct ancestor, it gave him a real buzz. Imagine being descended from a personal friend of King James I of England and VI of Scotland. Imagine that his forebear was a Chaplain-General, leading scores and scores of the first Ulster-Scots settlers to these shores. And imagine that he built and lived in this very house.

The electric wasn't connected up again into the tea-room, but without curtains it was still light enough to step down onto the stone flags. A shock ran up David's arm. In the corner, sitting on a high-backed chair, was Dan Lockhart – or his double.

'Hello?' David said, half expecting another death-defying look. A 'look' he sure got. From Dan's small piercing eyes came a bolt of timeless assault. He didn't know if it was good or bad, but it had the power of a stampeding horde, an unstoppable tribe with invincible strength. David tried to speak to ask him who he was, but nothing would come out.

'An quhat would you be after in this place?'

David found himself sitting in the corner alongside Dan. It was a good question, but open to different interpretations. 'What do you mean?'

'That's up tae yersel. Are you Mr. McGill?'

'Yes, David Magill.'

'I thocht so. It's your son Captain James I was really wantin tae see.'

David was just about to say he had no family, but an ecstatic feeling of total understanding came over him. He knew he was becoming 'possessed' by the Rev. David McGill … *and leant forward to poke the dying fire back into life. A shower of smoke and sparks like a pillar of fire rose up the inside of the massive ingle canopy they were sitting under. He felt strangely at peace. He reached behind him to the window sill for another taper of dipped rush stem to re-light his clay pipe. Mission accomplished, he snuffed out the taper and laid it carefully down on the low stool beside him with its smoking end overhanging the black wood.*

'Quhat else could I dae?' David McGill said in a reverent tone. He was completely confident now that he had done his Father's will in leaving Easterton to his offspring in perpetuity. It was a clever contract, and he was confident that his own earthly father, who had been Lord Advocate to King James, would have been proud of him.

'Thon guid wife o yours didnae let yer bed grow coul oniehoo.' Dan said.

'Na, my bed nor my pulpit.'

The Rev. James Montgomery from Montrose, a 'far-oot freen' of the Laird o Newton and the Ards, and a fellow Chaplin-General of the Laird's (along with David) in the early 1600s, took over David's position as curate of the Newton and Kirkreeba Church in the same year as David's 'lang' illness ended in 1633. To cap it all, the Rev. James Montgomery had then married his widow Elizabeth in the same year, for she was the Laird's niece and not to be left unsupported.

'Dae ye think I cudnae see that comin?' David said, smiling but not amused. 'I'm damned if I was gonnae let him sit in this hoose an lord it over my ain twa boys as weel.'

'Naethin guid ever come oot o Montrose, that's for sure,' Dan said.

'I knowed it frae the time we were at King's College thegither in Aberdeen.'

'The deil was crouching at yer door a lang while,' Dan said, 'an he wasnae short o money.'

'Richt,' said David, 'sae he'd nae need o Easterton an Easterhill.'

'But yer twa lads. They followed the bloody Duke o Montrose agin the Covenanters.'

'That was after my day.'

Rev. James Montgomery was expelled from his charge at Kirkreeba in 1643 by the Scotch Covenanting Army in Ulster for his 'refusal to renounce the Service book and swear the Covenant,' but when he threatened the 'Moderator' of the new Ulster-Scots Army with a cudgel, his living was restored. He was a man of substance, and would have nothing to do with those who wanted to replace the Established Kirk with the 'commonality' of the Solemn League and Covenant. The remnant of the Magill family was one with him on that one, and in 1637 when the would-be Presbyterian exiles sailed for America in the Eagle Wing, Captain James Magill and the Rev. James Montgomery were notable for their absence.

'The main thing,' said David, 'was that Elizabeth had tae make her choice – stay here an leeve in this hoose wi her twa sins, or bide in Westerkirk wi her new man.'

When David came down for his breakfast in the morning, he no longer had a problem with the 'life-time only' condition of his inheritance. He understood now that it wasn't done for any strange religious reason, but because the Rev. David McGill didn't trust his wife to 'honour and obey' after he was dead and gone. And he had a good deal of sympathy for that.

With one mystery solved in his own mind, David was almost behaving normally again. He was talking to himself less, and even joined in conversations when out socially. But he still had a strange need to find another obsessive quest for knowledge about some aspect of the Orange Tree Tea Room. And there was another change going on in his head. Before this, when he started to think about the history of the place, his mind would keep turning to the help he might get from Jeannie, and then it would move quickly on to what else he might get from her. But now when he saw Jeannie, instead of his heart jumping at the sight, it only made him think of what other historical information she might have.

'I still would love to know how the Orange Tree got its name,' David asked Jeannie. She shrugged her shoulders, but David could see that she knew more about it than that. A more direct approach was required. 'When did the tea-room first open?' he asked.

'I don't know,' Jeannie said truthfully. 'There's yin letter fae William Magill in Sooth Africa aboot echteen an sixty. An that was definitely before it was opened. Wait til I get it, for it says somethin aboot the renovations.'

The first thing David spotted was the stamp on the envelope. 'There ye are,' he said without even reading the letter. The Stamp was from the '*Oranje Vrij Staat*', and it had a picture of a stylised orange tree right bang in the middle. He really was turning into an incredible historian with his brilliant detective work. Just when that Robert Hugh Magill had been doing all his alterations and was about to open his new tea-room, hadn't Cousin William written to him from South Africa and, without even knowing, suggested the perfect new name.

'You could be right,' Jeannie said. David could feel what he thought was a glow of admiration coming from her. In fact, she was hardly able to disguise her feeling of superiority over this naïve, Ulster-American blow-in. His simplistic explanations of things that he didn't fully understand could be summed up by his half-baked interpretation of the orange tree. Did he not even know that the Dutch used the orange tree as a symbol for the House of Orange? One thing was for sure, he had never heard the song, 'The Old Orange Tree.' She even had the words of it in the file along with the letters and other loose, one-page, miscellaneous documents. 'But that,' thought Jeannie, 'I'll keep for a rainy day.'

Chapter 8

What's in a Name?

Kay was worried about David's increasingly odd behaviour. He was turning in on himself more and more, especially when they were in other people's company. It was lonely enough coming to live in Kirkreeba without her losing just about all meaningful communication with her husband. And as if the culture shock wasn't enough, there was the language barrier as well. But at least everyone could understand *her* – her home country and Hollywood Standard English had seen to that. 'What is my purpose here, Lord?' she frequently prayed, for without knowing what that was, it was so hard to plan David's future too.

Gumry was being quite difficult as well. Like many of the native inhabitants, he professed some sort of faith and indeed he even seemed to have an interest in religion. But to Kay it all appeared to be riddled with idolatry. She knew just how the foreign missionaries must have felt when, after years of work among the tribesmen, they found the converts still believing in witchcraft and medicine-men. Just when Kay thought she had talked Gumry into attending a bible-study session, he would make some excuse and not turn up. The problem seemed to be the involvement of third parties and a sense of letting his friends down. How could committing your life to the Lord involve a betrayal of your tradition? Kay couldn't understand it. But if it was tied up with tribal loyalty to a denomination, or a church building or a religious order, then those demons had to be faced down. The answer had to lie in somehow breaking free from these traditional albatrosses round all their necks. A neutral venue had to be found – but surely it was there already. The Orange Tree Tea Room would be at their disposal as soon as Gumry's work was done. 'That work,' she thought, 'is maybe service enough.' The tea-room's location at the old and original gate-way to the Abbacy was highly symbolic too. She imagined the challenge to visitors – 'what brought you here?'

Kay's idea of the Orange Tree Tea Room as an 'Orange Tree Christian Centre' didn't strike Gumry as being necessarily a contradiction in terms, but he wasn't comfortable with it at all. It was just a bit of a daft notion, something she would grow out of when she learnt more of their ways and the richness of local history and culture. After all, that was what brought the day-trippers – not religion.

'Ye know there's pairts o the oul flare is boased?' Gumry pointed out to David, stamping with his foot on one of the old exposed stone flags of the tea-room floor. The echoing, hollow sound reverberated round the room.

'D'ye think there's an entrance to a cellar down there?' David asked. They exchanged excited glances like boys about to launch into an adventure. Gumry remembered the old stories about a tunnel between the Abbacy and the 'Haw' as Orange Tree House was once called.

David was remembering something different – that Dan had told him one night about the 'answer' being 'richt under where ye're sittin.' From that moment an archaeological partnership was born.

'Should A lift her?' Gumry asked, stamping again with his heel on a flag in front of the blocked-up hearth.

'Fire ahead,' David said. 'Have you a crow-bar?'

The operation only took a few minutes, and once prised up, the heavy stone slab could be slid over the rest quite easily. But what a shock the two tomb-raiders had when they saw what they had discovered! Four or five gleaming white skulls of unknown beasts lay packed tightly together in a shallow pit. If anything ever looked pagan, this was it.

'They're horses' skulls,' Gumry eventually said. But that explained very little.

'Put the stone back,' David said, 'before Kay sees it, or she'll go mad.'

This find was to remain a secret between the two men for months, and the focus of many a wild theory. It was also the spur to more archaeological activity as David spent the next few sleepless nights seeking more insight from Dan. The source of his inspiration he kept to himself, but David eventually declared the skulls a 'sort of sound-box, like a fiddle case,' and not what they were looking for at all. Gumry was not convinced. 'But it shows,' David argued, 'that the room was built for singing and dancing, or some sort of public place.' Gumry felt something pagan going on, and at best it removed any further notions he might have had to search for buried tunnels, secrets or treasure.

'What possessed ye tae go hoakin aboot in there?' Jeannie asked Gumry. There was a touch of anger in her voice.

'Possessed, me? Mair like thon room's possessed,' Gumry said. 'It scarred the leevin daylights oot o me.'

'Was there onie writin on the back o the stane ye liftit?'

Right enough, thought Gumry, it was aboot the size of a head-stone. 'I cudnae say,' he said, 'we never couped it over.' It was a disturbing thought for him, those images of mortality under the tea-room floor, like a warning of some sort.

Kay wanted to keep the old stone floor in the tea-room, even thought it was below street level and would involve steps down in. 'Could you not raise the floor level and set them back?' she asked Gumry. He made an excuse about building regulations, and ordered in the timber to cover up the demon-possessed underworld as quickly as possible. If Kay was disappointed because she had been thinking with added excitement about her vision of the tea-room's future, David was equally disappointed, although in his case it was because of his frustrated quest to explore the tea-room's past.

Through the back rooms behind the tearoom, an old heavy-framed door led into a projecting, back stair tower. The spiral stone steps led up at the back corner of the house to each upper floor. Small slit windows overlooked the yard, and from outside at the back you could easily see how old that part of the house was. David, once the stone floor in the tea-room was covered in again, was determined not to be outdone and turned his attention to this part of the house. At the bottom of the back stairs was a small porch with an outside back door that opened out along the back of the dwelling. The floor of the stair tower was laid with stone flags, but in behind the spiral stairs it seemed as if there had once been steps going on down. 'Here,' thought David, 'is the way down to the cellars if ever there was one.' And the floor had a hollow, 'boase' sound here too.

The next few weeks saw David engaged in another one-man, archaeological excavation. But the cellars were to prove elusive yet again. Under the stone flags were criss-crossing iron bars, set in place to cap a well. It was not what David expected to find. As he lifted the flat stone, he could hear grit and dirt falling into water, so the black hole he had revealed was certain proof that his discovery was of some significance. A well was not what first sprung to David's mind. He thought immediately that it was the flooded cellar, and that was what was in his mind when he brought both Gumry and Kay to inspect it. Kay's torch didn't work, so Gumry nipped home for his industrial strength one, fully expecting it to reveal the puddle-ridden floor of a tunnel leading to the Abbacy. But Kay had already felt the curving stone side wall by the time Gumry returned. 'I think it's a well,' she said, as Gumry swept its side walls with his torch in a vain search for the opening that would prove his theory. 'I think ye might be right,' he eventually said, grudgingly.

At least their latest find was not something that might have sinister undertones, like the horse skulls. In that respect the well was neutral as far as Gumry was concerned. But Kay saw everything in a different light. She had largely given up on explaining things to David. Now it was Gumry who was proving a useful sounding board for her plans and ideas.

'Back home,' she explained, 'we had a wonderful pastor who opened a place he called the Garden Gate as a centre for …' She hesitated to think of a term that wouldn't make Gumry take an instant dislike to the idea. Homeless, unemployed, down-and-outs, drunks, drug-addicts, victims of abuse, disturbed, inadequate, even demon-possessed folk that only had one thing in common – they needed to be saved and turned into respectable churchgoers. '… Christian outreach,' she said to finish her sentence with exactly the effect she was trying to avoid.

'What's that got tae do wi the tea-room?'

'It's all about signs and miracles,' Kay said, 'for Pat's work at the Garden Gate sure saw some lives changed.' Realising that she wasn't answering Gumry's question, she tried once more to ignite some enthusiasm for her vision of the tea-room as a version of the Orange Grove Garden Gate project. 'The Garden Gate was really the gateway to a real full Christian life, like the gate to the Garden of Eden – you know – the Way – to the Tree of Life.'

Gumry couldn't connect to what was going on in Kay's head. Not that he had no interest in his own destiny in this life or the next, but whatever went on in Orange Grove, it sounded from Kay's lips more like a shut gate than an open way to him.

'What's that got tae dae with the tea-room?' he asked the self-appointed gate-keeper again.

'Can't you see the signs?' she asked, warming to her task. 'The 'Well' – that speaks for itself doesn't it? The 'Tree' – the Orange Tree Tea Room – that's been obvious all along to me. Even the skulls – Golgotha – the Place of Skulls isn't it? I just know all this was meant to be.'

Gumry's mind turned to the most disturbed and hurting soul he knew, next to himself.

'Jeannie,' he said, 'looked after her da for the best pairt o ten years in this hoose. Where daes she fit in tae yer plans?'

Jeannie's situation was not on Kay's radar screen, except for a nagging suspicion that she had designs on her husband. Of course she was concerned about Jeannie's 'loose' morals, if her reputation was anything to go by. But it had not occurred to her until now that Jeannie might have designs on her house and tea-room as well. 'If she commits herself to the Lord,' Kay answered, 'of course I'll involve her one hundred per cent.' Somehow, Gumry didn't see this as a satisfactory answer from any point of view.

Kay's tea-room project was trundling towards a precipice she hadn't been aware of. The 'orange tree' would never be seen in Kirkreeba in the same light as Kay's Californian dream. And if it wasn't going to be seen as just an ordinary fruit tree, it was never going to be taken to represent the 'Tree of Life' in Genesis and Revelation. As a name and as a symbol, the 'Orange Tree' had other 'religious' connotations in Kirkreeba.

Tam McClay had shown a few design sketches of the murals and orange-tree frieze for the refurbished tea-room to Kay. It wasn't exactly what she had in mind, but she wasn't quite sure what she wanted anyway.

'More plants and trees certainly – a bit like a garden in paradise?' Kay said, watching Tam intently to see if he had any idea what she meant.

'A could dae Adam an Eve under the tree if ye like,' Tam

said, half joking – but he had seen the like on many a banner. Kay thought that was another sign, but no, she thought, that would be too much in the customer's face.

When Tam showed the sketches to Jeannie, the design wasn't exactly what she had in mind either. 'What aboot some lines o poetry or somethin in fancy writin roon the top o the walls?' she suggested.

'Would she no' be lookin some religious texts if ye pit that tae her?' Tam said, for Kay's reputation as being more than a bit 'gospel-greedy' was widespread.

'What's wrang wi some lines frae a sang? The Old Orange Tree would be perfect.'

That was a brilliant idea, thought Tam, although it might have to be gone through for anything in it that might cause offence. The chorus would do anyway, for all it had was: *'So let us join both heart and hand, and lovingly agree; For we're loyal branches of the old Orange tree.'*

There was no malice in Tam's suggestion, although the truth was that the idea – and the devious intent – had originated with Jeannie. David was immediately suspicious, and asked Tam for a copy of the whole song. 'A could sing it, but A couldnae recite it,' Tam said. 'A maun get the wurds frae Jeannie.'

The words went through several sifts by Jeannie to leave out any references that might be too politically incorrect. 'Tam, the first three verses micht be a wee bit … ye know, but the last three's fine. A've put them doon on two different bits o paper.' Tam took them home to read carefully and show them to Gumry.

'Ye cannae put party sangs up in there,' Gumry said, 'just think.'

Tam read out the first two verses. 'Right enough,' he agreed when he finished. 'But it's a guid sang.' He read it out loud again just for the enjoyment.

THE OLD ORANGE TREE

When William came to England, the King of it to be,
He brought a plant along with him of the Old Orange tree.
He planted it near London, so pleasant was to see,
When a few branches there sprung up and gave us liberty.

Twas on the walls of Derry, where the Orangemen did parade,
To fight King James and all his men, they never were afraid.
And with the sons of prentices, they happily did join,
To march and muster there in strength, on the north side of the
    Boyne.

When William went to Ireland, the Protestants to join,
He took the plant with him, and placed it on the Boyne.
And with his troops, courageously, he fought them one to three –
King James and his men were sore afraid when they saw the Orange
    tree.

The two lads laughed and cackled like crows at the thought of Kay's face if that was ever to get painted up on the walls of the tea-room. But when the fun was over, it was obviously a non-starter.

'Seriously but,' Gumry said, 'Ye could run wi the other verses aa richt.'

'A don't know,' said Tam. 'It's no' the right thing for visitors.'

'Ask David anyhow. See what he thinks.'

Tam read out the other three verses as if he was testing it out on David and Kay.

The seed of this old Orange tree got scatter'd up and down,
Till a few branches there sprung up, enough to rule a town.
It grew in summer season – Oh! Pleasant 'twas to see –
The winter season it came on and cropp'd our Orange tree.

The winter season it is o'er, the weather's fine and clear,
Our Orange tree will flourish in the spring time of the year.

WHAT'S IN A NAME?

Our Orange tree will flourish, for the root is yet alive,
For where there is one branch dropp'd off, we have engrafted five.

Now to conclude and make an end, and finish up my song,
Here's health and peace, long life and rest to all true Orangemen.
And let us live in unity, and evermore agree,
And on the Twelfth day of July see fruit upon our tree.

'If there isnae somethin amang that that's suitable, there's somethin wrang,' Tam said.

Gumry agreed. 'But it aa boils doon tae what the tree means.'

'Or what ye tak' it tae mean,' Tam said. 'Maist o the folk'll just be dropping in for a cup o tay.'

Chapter 9

Digging up the Roots

If Gumry thought that it was a bit of a joke to suggest putting up the words of an Orange song on the walls of the tea-room, David didn't see the funny side of it. Mind, he seemed to have lost his sense of humour altogether. Only now and then, when something was on his mind that involved him in having to speak to somebody, did he bother communicating at all. Kay thought it was just with her that he was so quiet, and that that was because David was unwilling to put any effort into their relationship. True, David's lights only came on when he was in Jeannie's company, or when he was chasing up some historical facts to do with his latest notion.

The Old Orange Tree ballad jarred with him, even though he had only been shown the last verses and they were fairly bland. But he had enough sense to realise what was going on, and that the Magills were in danger of being made fools of. 'Kay,' he thought, 'must never see this.' Gumry had gone and told her about the skulls, after promising not to, so keeping it from him might be a difficult task. The best solution would be a new name for the tea-room altogether. He would ask Jeannie her opinion. She wouldn't think too highly of Tam once she found out the nature of the stunt he was playing at. Indeed, it was her own family's good name as well that was at stake.

When he did tackle Jeannie about the song, David was taken aback by her reaction.

'What's wrang wi it?' she asked haughtily. 'What did *you* think the place was called after then?'

'Did your father and mother not think it was a bit …, you know?'

'A bit what? Father was as prood o oor history as any Magill.'

There was a bit of a dig in that and David felt he was being told off. He beat a hasty retreat back into his troubled shell.

David didn't expect to sleep much that night. He was pacing the floor with his head buzzing. This Orange thing was annoying him. Jeannie dilating her nostrils at him didn't help either. Kay was more of a mind with him on that subject at least.

'I was talking to Jeannie about the name of the tea-room,' he said as he dived into his pyjamas.

Kay looked up over her glasses from the book she was reading in bed. The only thing that registered was that David had brought that woman's name into the bedroom, so she silently returned to her book with a dismissive shrug.

David settled down for the night into the rhythm of his churning thoughts. Even if the Orange Tree Tea Room did go back a hundred years or so, that part of the family history wasn't all that old. Not compared to the age of the house anyway. It must have got its 'Orange Tree' name after the renovations in the 1860s. In a perverse way, Jeannie had even told him proudly about the other side of the local tradition – the 'turn-oot' of Kirkreeba men in the 1798 rebellion. And that was against the Orange Militia. 'One thing,' he kept telling himself, 'I know for sure. The Magill family history began here, at the head of the Scotch settlers, nearly a hundred years before the Boyne or King Billy or any thought of remembering 1690.'

Some time later, a cup of tea was called for, if David was going to think up a suitable new name for the tea-room. 'Something to do with the Abbacy,' he wondered, as he came down the stairs. That at least would keep Kay happy – and the day-trippers, who only came to see the ruins anyway. But the locals would need to be weaned off their 'Orange' tree. A hard enough task if Jeannie's reaction was anything to go by. Maybe the new name would have to appeal to their Ulster-Scots roots in a different way.

The autobiography of the Duke of Montrose he had ordered through the post was in the new back kitchen behind the tearoom. Before he got to it, he spotted the copy of the old 1625 map of Kirkreeba. He forgot about the book momentarily. Inspiration was so near, he could feel it. 'There must have been a million things that happened here in the early days. I feel it in my bones,' he said out loud.

'It's in yer banes aa richt.' … David turned and nodded in agreement with the man who was standing in the back doorway. 'Ye're nae different than thon son o yours,' Dan continued.

'Ye cannae pit the blame on me for ocht Hugh done,' said David McGill, 'A toul ye the Covenanters came here lang after my day. An the same goes for the baith o them.'

'Ye daen the best ye could, but the boys' mither defied ye in death as weel as quhan ye were leevin.'

'Ay, she reared them tae be true tae her ain side o the hoose.'

'Huh,' Dan said, 'Not that there was that big a difference.'

'There was nae splits in the Kirk in my day. A hoose divid agane itsel cannae stand in mair ways than yin.'

'But quhaniver the splits come, they came wi a vengeance,' said Dan. 'An aa yer wills an testaments an bonds in laa couldnae stop them, could they?'

David McGill fell silent again, like he often did in those last painful years of mental illness when he watched his wife Elizabeth drift away from her contracted marital duties. He had left everything to James, his oldest son, but as a caution, made provisions for his younger son, Hugh, and the Abbacy Kirk to act as 'owerseers' of his estate.

'Ye never dreamt that Mr James Montgomery would tak' ower in yer pulpit as weel as yer bed,' Dan said.

'Na, but he never leeved in the hoose. An then come the wars an he was pit oot by the Carrick Covenanters. They were just a thrang o wreckers. Pittin Mr. James oot o the Abbacy Kirk was the yin guid thing they did.'

'Ah,' said Dan, 'the wars. That was the stairt o it. It wasnae lang before Mr James was Chaplain tae the Laird's regiment, an yer twa boys at his side as captains.'

'A couldnae hae seen that comin,' said David, 'the wars or the alliance.'

'If they had left it at that, it micht hae been aa richt. Instead o gangin aff tae fecht wi the Duke o' Montrose an him butcherin the Covenanters in Scotland.'

'Montrose wasnae that bad.'

'Tell that tae the yins roon here. It aa boils doon tae the bishops.'

'The bishops?'

'Ay, if ye dae awa wi the bishops, the lairds an the kings would faa wi them,' said Dan.

'I'll go alang wi ye there. The Kirk an Croon is the thing, or the deil rules.'

There was another thoughtful silence. 'A bit o a mess, is it no'? A never thocht it would aa come tae this.'

'Quhat-way? The Presbyterians splittin the kirk, an daein awa wi the bishops – or yer ain flesh an blood fechtin agin it?'

'Baith,' David answered. 'I was prood o the stand they took agin the Presbyterians, but it was mair the way they aa joined up agin me. An quhan they took Mr. James Montgomery for their new faither!' He shook his head at the thought of how sure he was that his carefully laid plans were watertight in law. But there was no accounting for the new Trustees plotting with his own son and heir to oversee the thwarting of his will. And then it happened again and again down the years.

'It's a lang road has nae turnin,' Dan said, 'but ye cannae turn the tide o history quhan it's spirit's no' wi ye.'

*'Quhat spirit are ye talkin aboot? The Halie Spirit or the will
o the people?'*

*'Baith,' said Dan with a piercing look that had the screams of
a hundred martyred covenanters buried in it.*

For the first two weeks in June, Kay noticed that David's
condition had been getting worse. He wasn't eating, and although he wasn't sleeping well either, he wouldn't get out of
bed at all some days.

'I've got an appointment for you at the doctor's,' she said
as she stood at the foot of their bed one lunch-time with her
hands on her hips in an assertive pose, doubly effective because
of its total lack of sympathy.

'What about 'The Crown,' he asked, 'is that not the answer?'

'The answer to what?'

'Instead of the 'Orange Tree.'

It was a well thought out answer to the problem of finding
a new name for the tea-room that wouldn't upset Dan and his
sort. And it had a sort of religious connection as well. But such
subtleties were completely lost on Kay, who didn't know there
was a problem with the name in the first place.

Of course, there was one big problem Kay could see. David's
behaviour was getting more and more abnormal and she would
only be able to cover it up for a few more days unless he snapped
out of it.

David's appointment at the doctor's was for 9.45am on
Tuesday 24th June and Kay was surprised to see him up and
dressed in good time.

'Now, remember honey to tell him that you can't concentrate on things as well as you used to,' she said as he went out
the door.

The date was easy to remember, she told the police two days
later, for Gumry had said it was Midsummer Day. How could
she ever forget it anyway? The days, and then the weeks, passed

by without any sign of his return.

At noon on the 24th, which indeed proved to be the longest day of the year, Kay had rung the health clinic to see if David was still there. 'No,' they had said, 'Mr Magill failed to attend.' With a mixture of concern and annoyance swelling up in her, Kay had convinced herself that David had gone down to the bowling club on some research project that had grabbed his fancy. He would probably be down there with his head buried in a book, or be talking to Jeannie.

'He went out to go to the doctor's this morning,' Kay told Gumry, 'but he didn't turn up, and I assumed he would be down here?'

'No,' Gumry said, 'I've seen nae sign o him, doon here. What aboot you, Tam?'

'Na,' Tam said, 'an he' hasnae been wi Jeannie – for she's been wi me aa mornin.'

That was a bit of a relief for Kay, but not much. 'Where could he be?' she said with a worried tremble in her voice.

'Ach dinnae worry,' Gumry said, 'sure ye know David. He'll be off on some investigation or other.' Trying to be helpful, he added, 'I'll go an get Jeannie. She'll know.'

Of course, Jeannie didn't know, but her concern only became as serious as Gumry's the next day. 'It just puts me in mind o the way my da went,' she said to Gumry. 'A feel sorry for Kay – now there's a thing ye never thocht ye'd hear me say.'

'When did you last see him?' a panicking Kay asked Jeannie on day three.

'He was doon here talkin about a new name for the tea-room.'

'A new name?' Kay parroted back with her mouth open.

'Ay, he wanted tae change it frae the Orange Tree tae a mair neutral yin. Like the 'King James I,' or 'King James's Tree.' He liked the idea o callin it after the king that started the planta-tion – when the Magills came over tae Ulster in the first place.'

'And when was he going to discuss that with me?' Kay's stress was beginning to take its toll.

Gumry could see that Kay was upset by Jeannie's manner.

'Oh he was,' Gumry assured her quickly. 'He thought you would like it because o the King James Bible.'

Kay was not convinced. 'So what did you tell him?' she asked Gumry.

'I told him he was daft. Folk roon here only know aboot the yin King James, an that's the other yin that we hunted over the Boyne.'

Gumry felt guilty when he remembered his last conversation with David. He might as well have hit him between the eyes when he had said to him too that folk would think it would be better calling it the King Billy Tea Room. Off David slunk home, with his tail between his legs, and that was the last Gumry saw of him before he went missing.

An awful fear began to grip him, imagining where David might be or what he might have done to himself. The only decent thing he could do was to try and keep Kay from having the same thoughts.

'Did your da ever try an hurt himsel'?' Gumry asked Jeannie when Kay was out of sight.

'A never knowed him to dae ocht like that, but he needed watched, mornin, noon an night.'

'Ay, specially at nicht,' Gumry laughed. 'D'ye mind the nicht he come oot in his dressin gown through the abbacy ruins an ontae the bowlin green in the moonlicht? We aa thocht it was a ghost.'

'I didn't know aboot that. He was a big worry at the time an I wouldnae wish it on my worst enemy.'

Gumry felt shamed. He knew there was a deep, good side to Jeannie's nature. But they had never really talked, even when he was in and out of her house all the time before the new

Magills arrived. 'Ye had it hard. D'ye think David's goin the same road as yer da?'

'A wudnae like to say it's in the Magill genes,' Jeannie joked without smiling, 'but there's a sort o pattern that goes back tae the very first o them.' She saw that Gumry was looking at her strangely. 'But just among the menfolk,' she added with a smile and placed her hand on Gumry's arm. He felt warm and comforted by that gesture, although he wasn't the one in need of it.

'Or maybe it comes wi the property. Ye know, stress an that.'

'Or it's a curse, mair like,' Jeannie said in all seriousness.

Now they were talking like real close friends, Gumry felt a warmness of physical attraction descend. This feeling was what he had wanted, and never had, in his short marriage, but that wasn't to say he was ready for any advance into that territory. He did, however, feel inclined to venture into subject areas that had been too personal to talk about before.

'D'ye miss leevin there? In yer ain hoose?'

'Na, not really,' Jeannie said, not knowing if she was lying or not. 'But A would be tellin lees if A said A wasnae bitter.'

'But, sure, he disnae really own it anyhow. Daes it no' fall tae the next in line, an him wi nane o a family?'

'Ay, sort of.'

'Is there nae new laas tae gie you yer richts as a woman an Hugh Magill's dauchter?'

'Look, Gumry,' she said looking intently into his eyes, 'for seven years I had fu' ownership as trustee an ward an guardian o my father. An A never got yin pick o pleasure oot o it.'

'What if David goes the same way, daes Kay get the same …?'

'The same life sentence?' Jeannie finished the question for him, 'for that's what it is.'

'Ay, well … whatever.'

'As a matter o fact, she disnae count,' Jeannie said.

Jeannie got a bit of pleasure out of that at least. 'She's neither a trustee nor a Magill in the eyes o the laa.'

'That's a bit hard on her,' Gumry thought to himself. He couldn't share any ill will towards Kay. This bitterness of Jeannie's was like a warning shot across his bows, for just as she was beginning to seem attractive again, he saw another side of her.

Just then too, Tam came over to their table in the clubroom. He put his two hands on Jeannie's shoulders and ran them down her arms in a very public display of familiarity. Jeannie slapped his hand loudly. 'Quit that, you!' she shouted as if she wasn't used to such behaviour. David's disappearance was having a sobering effect on everybody, as they retreated into their own shells of duty and social propriety.

'If anything has happened to him,' thought Jeannie, 'that poor woman Kay will be out on the street.' She made up her mind she would make an effort with her, sometime.

Chapter 10

The End of the Line

The waiting room was pretty much as David expected it to be, a few papers of the variety he never read and a host of glossy magazines on women's issues. He couldn't be bothered leafing among them. 'Mr. Sloan will see you soon, Mr. Magill, he's still with a client,' a girl's voice said from behind a high desk. David looked about the room. He was the only other person waiting, so that couldn't be bad. A bit different from the doctor's, where there could be eight or nine in front of you. He was glad he had decided to come to the solicitors when Kay had double-booked him into the doctors without consulting him. As long as he was on his own, he didn't mind waiting. It was restful, almost like a spiritual retreat. Time for meditation and no distractions. Solicitors never made house calls, like the doctors did. So their offices gave them an air of unchallengeable authority, infallibility almost. David felt strangely calm, almost forgetting the reason he had made the appointment with the Magill family solicitors in the first place.

'Mr. Magill? Sorry to keep you, come through please.' Mr. Sloan was standing with an enormous pile of files, so large he had to hold them in front of him with both hands. 'Sorry, I can't shake hands,' he said politely, 'take a seat.' Once he had thrown the large bundle on his desk, he reached round them to take David's hand and give it a single, firm shake. It reminded David of how an enormous bible used to be carried in to the pulpit in front of the one-man ministerial procession at his boyhood church. The Book of Rules gave such an added air of authority. Mr Sloan's files were well ordered and secured together, so that he could find any section he wanted straight away. David thought how good it would be if he had his papers so well organised, instead of scattered all over the place.

'What can I do for you? How have you and Mrs Magill settled in to your new life?'

'Fine, thank you. But I have a problem with my wife's plans for the Orange Tree Tea Room.'

'A problem? Well, what can I do to help?'

'It's the name. We've been getting it ready to re-open, but can we change the name?'

'Before I come to that. You do know that any improvements you make will be at your own expense, and your wife will not have any benefit from them after your death if they have not been approved in advance.'

'Approved? What do you mean? By who?'

'By the Trustees of the Magill Estate. It's all to protect your own interest, so that any investment you make by way of improvement is properly recorded, with the costs. It saves any wrangles after you go.'

'And if I do have that all down, the money comes back to my wife?'

'You can leave it to whomever you like – your wife or anybody else's wife for that matter.'

'So, Kay can only stay in the house as long as I'm alive?' David asked with no sign of emotion on his face.

'Well, more or less, unless you become incapacitated, and have to have your affairs managed by the estate. Like your predecessor, Hugh Magill. But it would probably be better for Mrs Magill if you didn't hang around for too many years like that.' Mr Sloan's idea of humour didn't appeal to David.

'But say I was … I needed looked after, surely it would be my wife,' asked David.

'I dare say she would, but the estate would be in the care and custody of the Trustees.'

'Who's that?'

'Well, providing the curate is happy to leave it to her as he did before, it would be Mrs Jean M'Clure, formerly Miss Jean Magill.'

The realisation that Jeannie was in such a position of potential influence, if not power, came as a bit of a shock to David. Not as much of a shock as it would to Kay, he thought. Maybe in his case it was more of a pleasant surprise.

'But what was it you wanted to ask me?' Mr Sloan asked David. For a minute he couldn't think what it was he had come for. 'You said something about the name?'

'Oh yes,' said David, 'presumably we don't need the Trustees permission to change the name of the tea-room to something like the 'Crown'?'

'Indeed, you do,' Mr Sloan replied. 'Of course, it can be done, but it means the title of the property has to be changed in some of the legal documents. Otherwise, imagine the confusion you will leave for your successor. I can do it, of course, if all parties agree.'

'So, basically you're saying that if Jeannie M'Clure agrees, there is no problem.'

'No, not quite, but if she does agree, then it can be done.'

David was left in a greater state of turmoil at the end of his meeting with Mr. Sloan than he was at the beginning. 'The Crown' didn't seem so convincing when he said it out loud. Jeannie would know he only wanted to get away from the 'House of Orange' association with the tea-room's name. She would take the side of the locals and stick her heels in just for badness, if not for tradition. But there was another way. If only he could get the message across that the 'Orange' thing was only a recent innovation. It didn't exist until at least a hundred years after the Magills arrived in Kirkreeba from Scotland. It was a matter of education, of raising the profile of the early Ulster-Scots. He had to prove, and he could, that the real 'Invincible' heroes of Kirkreeba were those early pioneers he had gathered so much information on. And then he had to get his message across.

As he walked back into the city centre, David's head was buzzing. He felt disturbed in the back of his mind about what the solicitor had told him, and that had upset him all the more because he had felt so good going in at the start. The thing he had to focus on was his research on the Magills before 1690. While he was up in town, he could try the library and see what they had. He felt a new good feeling as he made his way there. It reminded him of his morning walk to the book-store in Orange Grove. It was a long time since David had had that feeling of freedom.

In the Irish and Ulster history section of the reference library, David made a search through the indexes for anything on any Captain James Magill in the 1600s. The only Captain Magill he could find was a Captain Hugh Magill in the 1680s, long after Rev. David McGill's sons – James and Hugh – had both died. But just in case there was any connection, David checked the latter-day Captain Hugh out. The first mention was not what David wanted to find. Captain Hugh Magill was listed among the officers forming the Council of War in Londonderry to which the infamous Lundy read his letter of instructions from King William in 1689, at the approach of King James's army. The same Council of war then issued several proclamations of intent to defend the city and surrounding districts, and these were each signed by 'Hugh MacGill'.

Just as David was launching himself on the next phase of his enquiries – to see if this Hugh Magill was related to, or one of, the Kirkreeba Magills – the Library Assistant told him he had only ten minutes before closing and he couldn't order any more books. 'What is it you're looking for anyway?' the girl asked apologetically.

'Oh, it's to do with my family tree, the Magills,' he replied.

'You need to go to the Record Office, they'll have all that,' she said.

It was quite a walk to the Record Office, but exciting all the same. When David arrived there, he was hungry and annoyed with himself for being so stupid as to imagine it would be open in the evening. He checked the opening times on the notice outside and wondered where he could get something to eat. Maybe one of the guest houses he had passed could provide him with an evening meal and maybe bed and breakfast as well.

The Haven Guest House run by Ann and Alan Price was just what David needed. It was a family-run affair just like the sort of place he remembered staying in as a boy with his mother and father, and like nothing they had in California. They took a personal interest in all their guests, and were happy to accommodate a nice quiet man like David Magill.

Alan made conversation as soon as David checked in. 'We had quite a few Presbyterians staying with us during the week of the General Assembly, just two weeks back. It used to be we were completely booked out in June. Is this your first time with us?'

'Yes,' David said, 'It looks very comfortable.' He was slightly bemused by the comment, and even more so when Alan asked, 'Were you up for the Assembly yourself?'

'I'm not a Presbyterian,' he answered.

'Sorry, Church of Ireland?'

David nodded politely rather than explain he had no time for these labels. It was a bit bold, he thought to be asked his religion so directly, but nothing surprised him any more.

Alan Price checked the guest register again. Yes, it did say 'Rev. David McGill.'

'Is there a desk in the room I can use?' David said.

'Oh yes, I'll take you up. This is a very quiet area, so you'll not be disturbed.'

David Magill, whatever frame of mind he was in, would be a model guest with his quiet, meditative ways. The Haven, no matter how over-inquisitive the hosts were, was a model guesthouse in the circumstances. But it was going to be another busy night. There were questions he had to write down and sort out in his own head before the next assault on the Record Office in the morning. What a treasure trove of information that was proving to be. At times he half expected to look up from his notebooks and see Dan sitting beside him to put him right. But he didn't need him anymore. 'I knew it in my bones' he said to himself. *'I knew thon Hugh McGill at the siege of Derry was my grandson.'*

'And the other yin tae,' said Dan at his elbow, 'the mair James got cut off in his prime, baith brithers were boul Orange heroes.'

It was only a matter of weeks before the 1689 council of war at Derry when Hugh Magill's younger brother had been killed in the trenches on the Williamite side at Portglenone Brig.

'Nae compassionate leave in them days,' Dan said. 'Ye seen it in yer ain family Bible for yersel.'

'Ay. When things like that happen, it makes ye think. But ye cudnae complain aboot the twa brithers in those times, cud ye?'

David's notebook from his last three days' research was filling up. The richest source had proved to be the Hamilton and Montgomery Manuscripts, an antiquarian tome full of footnotes and bits and pieces about the two McGill grandsons of Rev. David McGill. Their mother was Jean Bailie of Kirkhaven Castle, just four miles from Kirkreeba, and her entries in the family Bible struck David like a hammer blow. But the historians account was matter-of-fact:

'James McGill served under lieutenant-colonel Shaw, who had charge of the trenches at Portglenone, and who being attacked, on the 7th of April, by a superior force of the Irish, was obliged to retreat after a gallant resistance in which several of his officers and men were killed.'

The Bible account was the one that spoke straight to the heart:

'Memer. – That my deir son Jeams McGill was murdred att Portglenone bridge with the barbarous Ierisse on the 7 day of apryll 1689, he being just tuintie yeire ould the night befor his death. I brought his bons hom in a box and lead them by his father.'

It was a temporary relief for David to discover that at least his other ancestor, Hugh Magill had managed to survive the Siege of Derry more or less in one piece. And then that he had survived the Battle of the Boyne on the 1st July 1690 too, actually fighting at the side of Rev. Walker of Derry who was not so lucky. But less than two weeks later disaster struck the Magill family for the second time at the Battle of Athlone. Again, the historians account was cold and detached, even when copied into David's notebook:

'The death of Hugh McGill at Athlone is noticed by Storey as having occurred on Sunday, the 20th of July, 1690. 'That day,' says he, 'one captain Mackgill, a volunteer, was killed at our battery with a canon shot from the castle.' – His death is also noticed by a brother officer, D. Campbell, in a letter addressed to sir Arthur Rawdon, and written from Carrickonsure on the 24th, four days after its occurrence. 'The lieutenant-general,' says the writer, 'broke ground and lost but about 14 men; the enemy raised a battery, and poor unfortunate Hugh McGill would needs go to see it, tho' dissuaded from it by every one; his arm and shoulder were shot from him by a cannon shot, of which he immediately fell dead, and not much lamented, because everyone condemned his going thither.'

'The baith o them,' said David, 'what a scunner. An the ink hardly dry in the family Bible.'
'That's the truth,' said Dan, 'poor woman.'
'She must hae been still in shock when she writ the next entry.'
'Thon Bible disnae lee, an that's the truth.'

Dan did not mean that any later additions to the inspired text carried the same authority as the sacred text itself. But he did mean to point up the poignant truth of a mother's short and despairing second verse:

'Memer. – That my deire sone hugh McGill was killed with a canon ball at the sedge of Achlone on the nynteine of Jullie 1690 he being in the thartie fyrst year of his edge.

In the space of two or three weeks, David had come a long way. He had forgotten what had brought him to the city in the first place. Even if he could have remembered, now it would just seem daft. Why the search had started, and what the search was for, didn't matter anymore. What he had found was the really important thing. To get to the base of the family tree felt like getting to the root of the matter. And what about finding an alternative name to the Orange Tree? David had no memory of feeling negative thoughts about that side of life in Kirkreeba. He was proud to be a Magill, instead of just being proud to be David Magill. It was a new-felt good to be at one with his tradition, his past. Even his forebears that now lived on in him made him feel good, or at least proud, if only he could connect better. If he could clear his mind of the clutter of today's trivia, it would seem almost as if they were back again, living history in his head. Birds had no such problems. They could just fly away. Without any head-clutter to block the signals, they could fly from continent to continent each year and find their home nest without having to do any thinking at all. He needed to know. It was like a drug. Would he know it all some day? *Not this side of the Jordan. Would the whole tribe be waiting on the other shore? What a thought. There would be no need for a Dan then, for he would instantly know them all, and all about their lives.*

It was on the morning of the first day of July that David came to the end of his line of inquiry with a jolt. He remembered his visit to the solicitors as if it had just been that same morning. It was time he was heading home, he thought, although he wasn't really aware of what time or date it was. When he left the Record Office for the last time that morning, he had already forgotten he had ever been there by the time he reached the bus station. But he hadn't forgotten what he had learnt about his roots. The discovery that brought him back to planet earth was not earth-shattering in itself. A simple legal settlement of lands on the Kirkreeba estates in 1691 had mentioned Hugh Magill as if no tragedy at all had hit the family. Typical, David thought, of the legal pen to ignore the fact that the person mentioned had just been buried. The first mention was a grant of peat cutting rights:

> '… the said William to have turbary, and leave to cutt three hundred load of turf in that part of the mosse which Hugh McGill, Innkeeper, had last year …'

The next question David had asked was what did Hugh want so much peat for anyway? As if reallocating Hugh's moss turbary rights wasn't disrespectful enough of a war hero, the document had a 'Schedule of Debts' attached, and heading the list was:

'Hugh McGill in Kirkreeba, Innkeeper, by two bonds, £27–12–00.'

It was this second reference to the late hero of Derry, Athlone and the Boyne as an 'Innkeeper' that made something click in David's mind. Hugh Magill had kept an inn in David's own house, in the Orange Tree Tea Room. What name had been on the sign? There was an inn-sign shown hanging from the Magill tower-house on the 1625 Raven picture-map that Jeannie had shown him. Now he knew what must have been painted on it – 'The Orange Tree Inn.' Mission accomplished. What else would such loyal servants of the King have called their hostelry?

It was late morning on the 2nd of July when David walked back into the bus station. How could he get his bus when the bus-company staff kept telling him to leave? At least they had waited til after midnight for the last couple of nights before throwing him out. He didn't really mind, for he felt so good in himself.

'Do you know my two grandsons fought and died for king and country?' he had told the station manager.

'Sorry sir, but …'

David pulled himself up to full height and interrupted the young whipper-snapper. *'At the Siege of Derry and the Boyne – both of them!'*

'A deadly combination, drink, religion and the silly season,' the station manager thought.

Chapter 11

To the Field and Back

It was the 7th of July, and exactly two weeks since David had gone missing. Nobody was counting the days but Kay anymore, although there was still deep concern the length and breadth of the Lang Raa. It had ruffled the feathers of the Kirkreeba Craas to such an extent that the police didn't regard their search as just a domestic affair. Some progress had been made, and David's visit to the Solicitor's on the day of his disappearance was the first discovery the police had made. That set everybody imagining the worst – maybe he had been settling his affairs before doing something stupid? But when cheques were being cashed, that was a big relief. The Haven Guest House was the best lead the police's missing-person search had got, but he had only been there until the end of June.

Kay went herself up to town to see Ann and Alan Price at the Haven. 'The *Reverend* David Magill?' she declared with a nervous laugh. 'If only,' she thought briefly, but it was a comfort that, even if he had had some sort of breakdown, he was obviously thinking about his eternal destiny. 'Especially,' she thought, 'if anything has happened to him.'

'He was … I mean, is … a model guest, working away on his devotions or whatever in his room and didn't bother a soul,' Ann Price said. 'I'm sure he's all right. You would have heard if anything had happened.'

Kay nodded and managed a polite, kind smile as befitting a minister's wife. She wasn't going to say anything more.

When she came home and told Gumry where she had been,

she left out the 'Reverend' bit. That was her personal bit of comfort. People had remarked on how well she was bearing up under the circumstances, and that she must have such inner strength. Gumry, on the other hand, knew that Jeannie M'Clure had been up to see the Solicitor on her own investigation into the affair. Gumry wasn't going to tell Kay anything about that. There might be implications depending on the outcome, and Kay had no idea that she might not be the lady of the house for much longer.

The new wooden floor that had been put in on top of the old stone flags in the tea-room, and the walls that Gumry had re-plastered were beginning to look old and dusty now that the work had ground to a halt. Even if David turned up back home now, it would take a while for Kay to retune her mind to the tea-room vision and get the ball rolling again. Gumry asked her about what work she wanted him to do next. Kay did try to think about it, just to have Gumry around the place for company. But she couldn't make up her mind.

'A'll hae tae get the stuff ordered an picked up before the yard shuts for the Twelfth fortnight,' Gumry explained.

'A fortnight?' Kay said, 'how do you usually manage yourself then?'

'Sure we're all off tae. It's the holidays, isn't it?'

Kay couldn't believe that the whole country seemed to close down for the Twelfth of July, but had too much on her mind to try and understand what the holiday was about. She had seen the 4th of July come and go without giving her own country's celebrations a second thought. Her loyalty was to her Lord, although in the States that didn't seem to jar in any way with her loyalty to the Stars and Stripes. When she saw this fixation with loyalty to a different flag all about her, literally, as it was just then, she felt strongly moved to replace it all with true religion. When she saw tribal religion all about her, she wanted to replace it with true spirituality. When she saw Old Testament tribalism all about her, she wanted to replace it with New Life testimony.

In the established denominations of Kirkreeba she had become a real non-conformist and dissenter. As far as Kay's negative attitudes to the churches were concerned, Gumry was broadly sympathetic, at least in principle if not in practice. But when it came to Kay's demonisation of the Orange tradition, assuming it was somehow bad and sinful just because it wasn't part of her culture, then he had to take exception. It was a real and unexpected source of tension between them, but not something to argue about. Gumry bit his tongue and said nothing when Kay told him they shouldn't be allowed to take over the whole road as the Invincible Heroes made their first appearance of the season. What did she want them to do – walk along the footpads of the Lang Raa behind the Star of Easterhill Pipe Band? That first outing was for the unfurling of their new banner, and it was a lovely turnout, Gumry thought. Kay's negative comments made him flare up inside with hurt and anger. But he turned away thinking, what a cheek! That was the Christian thing to do. She was obviously stressed-out because of her missing husband. But life had to go on, and the Twelfth wasn't going to be cancelled in Kirkreeba or anywhere else just because some self-centred people didn't like it.

It was a bright and glorious Twelfth morning in Kirkreeba, but Kay was not alone in feeling alienated from the early morning stirrings. Gumry's ex-wife Annie had been stumping round the house in a huff for two or three days, slamming doors and throwing herself into chairs to stare out the window and not speak even when she was spoken to by her mother and younger brother Lee. The only thing of Gumry's that Annie had kept when she moved back to her parent's house was his surname, and that was just a reminder to all and sundry that she was the injured party. The only one, she thought, that had taken her side was her father. Stuart Hamilton had left the lodge when no action was taken against Gumry for his hochmagandy with Jeannie 'Magill.'

'A'll no sit under him, wi him in the chair, nor walk behin him,' he said, when some of the senior officers paid him a wee visit. 'Naebody treats a dauchter o mine like that. Naebody,' was his parting shot to the delegation, to Annie's immense satisfaction.

Annie's problem with the rest of the family began with her mother. 'Sure, it was just a bit o nonsense,' she had said, 'your place isnae here, it's back wi yer man.' Annie couldn't believe that her own mother had taken that attitude, and not be happy to have her back at home. Of course, in a sense she was, but only let it show in small things.

Annie's brother Lee was just being Lee, a fifteen-year-old lad with a natural dislike of having suddenly been burdened with three people in the house determined to boss him around.

The immediate cause for Annie's concern with Lee was the re-emergence in her house of the Magill tartan, in the shape of Lee's band uniform. The very sight of the kilt made Annie's blood boil. 'Ye're not for puttin that on ye again, are ye?' she snapped at her brother in a rare outburst of communication. 'What d'ye want me tae wear?' but it was too late, for Lee was talking to the back of door again.

There was no mistaking the Magill tartan. It was a blaze of different colours – blue, yellow, white, green, black and red. Unlike most other kiltie bands that had uniforms in a tartan which gave off a dominant red or green hue from a distance, Kirkreeba's 'Star of Easterhill Pipe Band,' as it was called on the bass drum, could be spotted a mile off. Its distinctive multi-coloured spray was like a Dutch flower garden, a riot of clashing colours as loud as the pipes themselves. When Annie saw Lee cleaning and preparing his stuff on the eleventh night, she realised that the next day wasn't going to be treated in the Hamilton household as a total snub to Gumry. The house stank with whitening and Silvo. Lee's black leather drum-belts were his trade secret. The boot polish was put on thick and a match passed over it till it just melted. This was an old army trick, so Lee's father had told him years back. The table was still covered with old newspapers the next morning at half six when Mrs Hamilton raised her son from his bed.

''Ye'll be needin a guid breakfast theday son,' she said.

In a few minutes the frying pan was spitting and flashing as the smell of bacon, soda farls, pritta breid and eggs heralded a new and special dawn. It was changed days since Lee was only about six years old and used to walk in a wee miniature uniform beside his father. Stuart was Drum Major in those days, and back then the rise and fall of father and son's matching big and wee maces in time to the swing of the band's step was a favourite for the town centre snap-shooters. But the smell of the Ulster fry brought all those happy days back to mind.

The band had their practices just out of town, in the upstairs lodge-room of Kirkreeba Orange Hall built on a plot of land donated by William Hugh Magill in 1881. Outside the hall that early morning, a few pipers were making their first sounds as Lee and Billy Close joined them after their proud, smiling dander out from the Lang Raa.

'Ye right, Hammie?' said Tam M'Clay to Lee. Tam was the stand-in Drum Major, but looked every inch the part – and he knew it. He made a mock inspection of Lee and Billy's turn-out, and wandered off on his rounds as he checked who else still had to come.

'What's that tune ye're playin Sam?' Lee asked one of the pipers pacing and playing up and down the side of the two-storey hall.

'It's an oul Chinese tune, Hammie,' Sam answered with a grin, 'called Choo Nin Up.'

Inside the hall, the wafting sounds of the pipes warming up and machine-gun bursts of side drums practising their attacks could be heard as background. Some of the bandsmen who were also in the lodge were in there too. Their uniforms seemed to give them a special status, but this was contradicted by the seating arrangements as the day was officially opened in due form. The marshalling arrangements were outlined and the catering and transport details reported. The final business concerned the arrangements for a cup of tea and dance in the hall at the end of the day. The supper and dance could well have been done without, but it was done as a thank-you to the band, so nobody dared to suggest that it be dropped.

It was the turn for the nearby town of Westerkirk to host the main demonstration, although it was not really the town but the Fair Hill outside the town which was the real venue. Like all Twelfth parades, the event might start near the town centre, but its real destination was always the 'field.' The Kirkreeba Invincible Heroes started the day outside the hall as they lined up behind the band and new banner. The turnout was good, both in terms of numbers and smartness, and the specially-decorated car was purring as old Ephie M'Clay was helped in by his sons Tam and Sammy.

'Just yin tune tae we get oot on the road,' Sammy shouted above the excited din to his brother at the head of the band, 'we want tae gie Dan and Eddie a quick first lift o the new banner.' The oldest and the youngest member of the lodge were to be given the privilege of the first 'Twelfth' carry of the new banner. As the banner poles were slotted into the leather straps and cup holders round the necks of the two, banner strings fore and aft were given to four 'juveniles.' Dan turned to his young partner Eddie and gave him a stern look. 'This is a great honour for you son,' he said, and smiled when he saw that the young man beside him did seem to appreciate what was being asked of him.

With a 'by the left' and a few sharp drumbeats to mark the step, they were off, suddenly, for it caught some of the lodge unawares. By the time they were out on the country road and the first tune had started up, the parade towards the Lang Raa was under way in fine style. Gumry had it worked out precisely. The first tune was to be 'The Old Orange Tree,' and then it was up to Tam to choose. That would give Dan enough time for a short lift of the new banner, and then they had to stop and let him into the official car alongside old Ephie. This strategy had the double advantage of not playing 'The Old Orange Tree' as they passed Kay and the tea-room. Not that she would know the tune anyway, but it was more a mark of respect with David still missing. In ten minutes they would be on the buses at the far end of Kirkreeba to take them to the main demonstration.

The sympathetic gesture of which tune to avoid playing when passing the Orange Tree Tea Room was completely lost on a tight-lipped Kay, as she watched them go past the door. She didn't return Gumry's white-gloved wave or his smile. A hundred yards on, Annie watched with even tighter lips. Gumry smiled at an imaginary friend on the other side of the street and pretended not to notice her.

Jeannie and Jack M'Clure had already got on the front bus with most of the other wives, girl-friends, supporters, weans and other assorted day-outers by the time the band and lodge reached the departure point outside the Duke o' Montrose. As the band and brethren piled on the second and third buses, the front bus was alive with a noisy excitement of the sort Jack didn't care for. Most of the people he would have considered friends were on the other buses. Jeannie got fed up talking across the front of her uninterested husband to some of the young wives across the aisle, so they swapped seats. Jack stared silently and impatiently out the window, and wondered how far they were going to have to walk from where the bus dropped them off.

Last year they took the car and had to park in a field that was miles outside the town. In Westerkirk the top end of the Main Street would be the best place to watch the parade, as long as all the best positions on front of the footpad hadn't been taken. There was no clearer sign of age than the foldout camp chairs Jack had brought to encamp on the front line looking up Meetin Hoose Brae as it twisted back up and out of town towards the school playing fields where the districts were to muster.

When Jeannie and Jack took up their positions, there were already folk three or four deep along both sides of the route. The buzz was constant as different heads craned to keep watch up the traffic-free brae for the first sight or sound of the men. It was much the same for over an hour. 'What time daes it start?' Jack asked for the tenth time studying his watch. 'Don't worry,' Jeannie said, 'Ye'll no' miss it.'

In the distance a faint chaotic rumble of thundering drums and other, through-other sounds could be heard. The rumble got gradually louder till there was no mistaking that the parade was on its way. Suddenly the buzz around them in the waiting crowd got louder, even drowning out the distant thumpeting. 'Here they come,' 'Ay, there they are noo.' Then, at the top of the brae, the first glinting of silver swords, pikes, flags, banners, uniforms and instruments appeared. The spearhead of the parade was a trickle of District and County Officers with their colour party, flags, drawn silver swords, bannerettes and guards. Jeannie watched the anonymous white amulets swinging in perfect military synchronisation, and then felt an almost sinful rush of excitement at the sight of the first band in its pride of place. The blaze of colour in the advance party was boosted at its heart by the bright, fire-brigade red uniforms of Westerkirk Silver Band. The trickle seemed to be pushed forward by a never-ending, surging wave. Westerkirk Chosen Few, as the host lodge for the parade, headed the local Number 3 District which was only beginning to emerge in full mighty strength round the top of the brae.

The Twelfth in Westerkirk was a brave and glorious day to all those watching and wanting it to be. The parade filled the streets wall to wall as far as the eye could see, pushing the crowd tight against the shop fronts. Jeannie felt there was something different, but couldn't put her finger on it. Maybe it was just herself, re-feeling that forgotten sense of one-ness with a people and a past. When she saw the Kirkreeba contingent, her heart leapt as the larger-than-life portrait of her father fluttered and glinted. It sailed proud between banner poles and cross bar with clumps of Orange Lilies and Sweet Williams tied with ribbons onto the silver-starred tops of the banner poles. She choked as she saw the ribbons were black. In fact she was so busy looking up that she missed half the band and Gumry and all her favourite men waving and calling to her and Jack. But she didn't miss the sound of the band. A tear of appreciation came to her eye as she heard the tune Tam had pre-arranged the band to be playing as they passed that spot. It was as if the entire parade was there to inspire and encourage her at the end of the worst year of her life.

After what seemed like an eternity, and dozens of pairs of Lambeg drummers, scores of flute and accordion bands, occasional oddity bands, precisely twelve pipe bands (for they were all compared and counted) and what seemed like hundreds of banners marking separate lodges and each telling a separate story, the last lodge trailed past bringing up the rear. The buzz of the crowd was different now, not as excited, and people discussed and shouted what next. Some stragglers went onto the road to follow their ain folk in the parade to the field. 'A guid turn-oot the yeir,' Jack said. He wondered if Jeannie would want to stay for the day or go back home early. They sat on for a while as folk brushed past and around. 'What noo?' Jack asked hopefully, 'is that it?'

'Sure, the day's just started,' said Jeannie, 'here's Number 4 District.' Sure enough, coming down the brae like another mighty outpouring from a well whose geyser blew once a year bobbed the next section of the parade. After another thirty minutes of Jeannie's chest being subjected to waves of bass drum beats that she could feel as much as hear, she could look back up the brae and see the massive sea of faces still coming as far as the eye could see. Her heart gave a tribal stir as she imagined it like a mighty river, with the banners bobbing and swaying forward as if they were a line of barge-sails from a fleet of boats. Only when the banners came close could she see the different scenes and names. Only when the marchers came close enough to see their faces did they come alive as individuals too. Thousands and thousands of completely different lives and stories, all in step with a single purpose, and clutching in their heads a unique word of scripture they had all received that very morning. Jeannie knew the form, but not the word. This year more than most it was all about memories for Jeannie; her father's painting on the banner among the host.

Hammie and Gumry were both foot-sair by the time they trudged with their band and lodge off the tarmac road under the 'Welcome Brethren' banner, and onto the muffled grass of the field. They seemed to keep on walking up and down over acres and acres of grass. They stumbled on behind a disintegrating drum corps of the band that was only held together by a persistent tap-tap-tap of the lead side drummer. All attempts at keeping in step were abandoned as the Kirkreeba squad struck off in a lone course to find its own picnic-spot- come-battle-station. A large oak tree growing in the far corner of the field was the designated spot.

'Pit yer pipes doon here, beside the drums,' called Tam. Once all the surplus baggage was stacked in a pile, the banner frame was carefully laid on top. The poles sat like cart-shafts on either side of the band's treasured armoury, and spread over all was 'The Late W. Bro. Hugh Magill, J.P.,' uppermost and keeping guard on the lot.

'Anybody that's no' hangin roon' for the platform resolutions, back here at half three shairp,' Tam and Gumry told their respective charges. The prospect of the return walk over the same distance wasn't to be contemplated till shoes were removed and a few hours breather given to scores of Kirkreeba pairs of socks.

Among the lost children wandering in and out the sitting, lying, standing and playing groups scattered by the hundreds across the field looking for their wards and picnic lunches, were bandsmen, lads, with open-necked uniforms released to show they were off-duty. Wandering bandsmen weaved in and out of groups of seated band girls, strutting their stuff in pairs and looking for 'a wee coort.' Rushing, sweating stewards and marshals dashed about looking for lodges that weren't where they were supposed to be. Among all these a few elderly gentlemen greeted each other in their Sunday best, looking remarkably cool in their overdressed states. A scruffy man approached them as if about to beg some loose change to visit the beer tent.

David McGill was nearly at the end of his historical quest. He could feel it in his bones again. The final connections were right here in the field, in the aftermath of the battle. Picking his way through the skailed bodies, weapons and clothing, he was heartened by the fact that there was no sight of blood, death or injury anywhere. He felt sure he would find his grandson Hugh alive and well after all. He was meant to follow this journey and change the course of history.

'Hae ye seen Captain Hugh McGill anywhere?' David asked a man in the uniform of a high-ranking officer.

'Where's he frae?'

'Kirkreeba,' David answered.

'Wha's he wi,' the Invincible Heroes?'

'Ay, that's richt.'

'They should be ower thonner at the big tree. Ask Gumry Caldwell if he's aboot.'

David picked his way through resting troopers, piles of pikes, swords and flags, and stumbled on past drummer boys by the dozen towards the oak tree. He froze, shocked, when he came to the Invincible Heroes encampment. The face on the banner – no! The name on the cover hiding the pile of bodies confirmed his worst fears – the late Hugh Magill! Distraught, he turned to find the commanding officer.

'Quhan did Hugh dee?' David asked Tam M'Clay.

'Hugh Magill? Did ye know him?'

'Ay ...' David hadn't got finishing his sentence before Tam recognised him.

'David Magill? Is that you?'

'Ay ...'

'Houl on. ... Gumry! C'mon over. Look wha's here – Mr. Magill.'

Gumry and the two or three others with him all came racing over to see for themselves.

'Is that you, David? Are ye all right?' Without waiting for an answer, Gumry shouted to some of the kilted bandsmen he saw walking towards one of the marquee catering tents, 'Hae ye seen Jeannie? he guldered, 'get her quick.'

Jeannie was sitting in the church marquee with Jack eating their 'sit-down' salad lunch when the news broke that David Magill had been found safe and well. She rushed out as if it were her own father. 'David, David, where have you been? Are ye all right?'

'Elizabeth?' the Rev. David McGill asked, 'I'm so sorry aboot Hugh, he's deid ye know.'

Jeannie was doubly shocked at David's physical and mental

state. 'You look wore oot,' she said, 'come on till we get ye a wee seat.' David was happy to accept this concern and allowed himself to be led off to a quiet corner of the Parish Church marquee.

'Hoo are we gonnae get him hame?' Jeannie asked Gumry. 'Should we no' let Kay know?'

'Hoo could we dae that? We'd better tak him back wi us.'

'Dinnae let him oot o yer sicht,' Jeannie said, 'an ye maun put him in the official car alang wi oul Ephie an Dan.'

'He's definitely rannerin, or he's loast his memory or somethin,' said Gumry.

'O coorse he is, why else would he hae gone missin?' Jeannie replied sharply.

On the demonstration's way back from the field there weren't as many folk lining the streets of Westertkirk as there had been in the morning. It was a sair trudge for them all. Gumry even toyed with the idea of volunteering to travel in the car along with David, just to keep an eye on him, but he had leadership to show in the ranks till the day was done.

It was left to Jeannie to take David by the arm back to Kay and his house when the convoy arrived back in Kirkreeba.

David was happy to leave Dan in the car with a wave when they reached the Lang Raa. They had both been strangely silent, but Dan didn't need to say anything for David knew that the unspoken word of shared hurt and grief was all that was needed. But there was some comfort in the triumphant homecoming to a heroes' welcome among the ordinary folk of the parish. The house was good to be back in. It seemed like ages since he had left for Athlone to find Hugh, and it was nice of his guidwife to come and meet him at the battlefield when she heard the news.

There were times following David's homecoming, when Jeannie called, that the Rev. David again took Jeannie to be his wife, Elizabeth. Then he understood fully why he was still in love with her. On those occasions Kay was just the housekeeper, and a fairly pushy one at that. But a man in his position knew how to keep her in her place.

'Elizabeth, tell this woman I'll take my supper in my room.'

When Jeannie wasn't around, Kay became Elizabeth, but with her it was the 'Elizabeth' that had betrayed David, not the one he still loved.

'Has thon blackguard Montgomery been roon here again?'

'No, honey, his work in the house is finished.'

'The deil himsel has possession o him. He must never take my place.'

Kay was alarmed to hear David talk about the devil before he shuffled off to his room muttering to himself.

Ye cannae fecht the deil if he haes a fit-houl in yer ain hoose. An in yer ain femily. I hae nae ither choice. I maun wrassle wi him thenicht. Whan she's sleepin. Thon throat will tell nae mair lees whan I squeeze him oot.

Chapter 12

An Upset House

Kay had a strong faith that involved an unshakeable belief in demons. This belief wasn't just in disembodied evil spirits, but in squatter demons that worked and lived in the people around her. This was, in some senses, a good thing. She didn't usually see bad people as bad, but like the King family back in California, as potentially good people in bondage to satanic forces. She had living proof of this in the counselling sessions she used to help Pat Mahood with at the Crossroads Fellowship in Orange Grove. The transformation of Anna King before her very eyes was amazing. Even later when Anna got pregnant and confessed her subsequent transgressions to the prayer group, it was a different state of affairs. She would have loved to have shared all this with David, but he wasn't involved in Crossroads and as far as she knew, he hadn't the slightest interest in people like Anna. Anyway, that side of things was strictly confidential and personal.

Back then even David seemed to have small demons that made him come up with excuses for not going to church. Kay also detected that in the Orange Grove bookshop he had another small demon starting to show itself. This one was the seed of original sin – to eat of the tree of knowledge. Through that book-learning, David was trying to master the universe around him, independently, and without reference to his Creator. David's interest in self-acquired wisdom was, as he saw it, more about discovering himself – who he was, where he had come from and why he was here. Surely, as David saw it, this was no sin. Kay could hardly argue against that at the start. His family history research was harmless enough till it became an unholy obsession. But now it was too late to quote scripture, although Kay had tried it anyway.

'Honey, the Apostle Paul warned against us devoting ourselves to myths and endless genealogies,' she had said when David first tried to share his exciting discoveries about the early Magills.

'It's not a myth,' he snapped back, 'It's in black and white.'

Kay gave him the silent treatment, so he continued. 'And it's part of the conditions of the will and legal ownership of our own house.' The sullen silence continued. 'Is that not important?'

'Paul says in his letter to Titus to avoid foolish controversies and genealogies and arguments and quarrels about the law, because these are unprofitable and useless.'

It was David's turn to give Kay the silent treatment, but it was more in anger than in hurt.

And then the demon took full control.

Kay didn't seem to ever acknowledge that any demons might try to take up residence in her own life. This was a real problem. It was her faith and principles that kept her apart now from any of the churches in Kirkreeba. She needed no excuses for not attending when shunning them was actually the right thing to do. Or so this wee small voice inside her said. Kay was convinced she had her own built-in radar for detecting evil spirits. Nobody was immune, not even the clergy – especially the local clergy she had met in her first trip round the local churches in Kirkreeba. She had developed an incredible sensitivity in that direction. Back in California, Kay had no memory of feeling that way about the other churches in Orange Grove. Certainly, Crossroads had been like an extension of herself, an immune sanctuary. But in Kirkreeba they were positively riddled with the anti-Christ. When David and Kay moved to Kirkreeba, she was taken aback to find that personal demons were all around her in other people. She had expected God to travel, but not necessarily Satan too. At least not just as quickly and clearly. Jack M'Clure was obvious – a sleazy slave to the demon drink. Tam M'Clay and Jeannie M'Clure were wallowing in lust, and the foul language on everybody's lips was perfect testimony to who their common master was.

All through the time David had been missing, Kay did get some sort of solace from Gumry. But then, in spite of her pleas, he chose to ignore her feelings. Instead, he decided to walk the broad road of damnation along with his legions of cronies on the Twelfth. It had seemed an affront to everything she held dear, that morning when the lodge came marching past. But it was all as nothing compared to the shock of having David returned to her by that same band of brothers. Dear knows, she thought, what he had been subjected to during that day-long orgy of strange primeval rituals. He was now fully possessed, and they were all to blame.

As one might expect, the Prince of Darkness seemed to rule David more completely at night than in the cold light of day. Jeannie had to come and stay most of the next few days until night-time, as she was the only person David would take directions from.

'Ye're no weel, David,' she said. 'I'm takin your shoes and clothes, in case ye wander off again. The doctor'll be here be in the mornin.'

'But I need my books and papers Elizabeth.'

'That's all richt. I'll get ye them, an a wee desk for your room.'

'Thank you my dear,' he said, glad to be home from his sad excursion. 'But what is to become of the Orange Tree Inn, now that Hugh is gone?'

Jeannie choked momentarily. It was just like being back looking after her father. In fact, she had to stop herself thinking

David was her father at times. She straightened up and said, 'Ye're exhausted wi your journey. Ye're not goin oot o this hoose till I say so.'

'What would I dae wi'oot ye Elizabeth. At least we won the battle. We must keep the name alive, for the sake of all them that fell.'

Alone in the house with David when darkness fell, Kay retreated to another bedroom she had decided to make her own. It was a thing she had sworn she would never do, but David got so aggressive with her when Jeannie wasn't around that she was nervous of being alone with him. The first night in separate rooms had been a last-minute decision, but now she had her own things moved in. The landing light was still on, so she opened her door to turn off the switch at the top of the stairs. David made her jump. He was standing there and swung round to glare at her.

'I know what you're plannin whenever I dee,' he said slowly and with menace, *'but I can stop ye in your tracks.'*

Kay jumped back into her room and shut the door. If only she had a lock. She held the door shut with both hands on the handle to stop it turning and her foot against the bottom of the door. It seemed like half an hour before she could see the line of light under the door from the landing light go out, but Kay stood on, frozen to the spot, listening for any sound at all.

After an eternity Kay went to her own bed, and sat with the light on reading, but not reading. When she was sure all was quiet, she turned out the bedside light. There was a faint red glow from her digital alarm clock – enough to see the outline of everything in the room. The large double-door wooden wardrobe that David had bought at an auction had one door that kept swinging open. Now filled with Kay's clothes, it was jammed shut with a piece of folded card. It had given her the fright of her life getting into bed, for her movement across the floor had dislodged the paper wedge and it had swung open behind her.

At 2:58 there was a sound, but that was all. At 3:18 the light appeared under the door, just for a second, and then it went out again. Kay got out of bed as quickly as she could without making a noise. She moved towards the door to hold the handle again, but before she could reach it, she saw it turn. Kay froze for a second as the door handle seemed to move, then stop, then turn a little more. Instinctively, she made for the wardrobe and pushed in through the open door to a clang of coat-hangers.

The door opened and the angry, unmistakable sound of David's excited breathing advanced in front of his silhouette towards Kay's bed. There he stood; studying the empty bed while Kay was sure her pounding, terrified heart was as loud as the drums on the Twelfth. She tried to flee through the open door, but couldn't move. David leant over the bed and prodded the covers to make sure it was empty. At this last chance, Kay tried again to run for it. This time she shrieked and ran at the same time, pushing David face first onto the bed before reaching the door and clearing the stairs with feet drumming like pistons down to the kitchen.

There was silence again. After an hour, Kay began to wonder had David passed out. Maybe he had fainted, or had a heart attack. She surely gave him a scare to match her own. But there was no way she was going to climb those stairs again to check him out. If she survived the night, she would take it as a sign to leave him, and Kirkreeba, and return home. It could hardly be a sin to divorce the devil.

When dawn came and the birds were singing, the horrors of the night seemed unreal. It was a lovely Sunday morning and a mile or so away Jack and Jeannie were preparing for their Sunday morning rituals in the tranquillity of Green Acres. Jack was dressed in his Sunday best, like a good Ulster-Scot, to enjoy his papers, have his morning glass, and maybe potter around the garden in a lazy way befitting his well-earned day of rest. Things were good for him at the minute, and in twenty-four hours they would be off to Spain for their annual post-Twelfth holiday. But the peace was suddenly disturbed by the sound of a car pulling into the drive-in front of their bungalow.

'Who the hell's this on a Sunday mornin?' Jack called back into the bedroom where Jeannie was setting piles of holiday clothes out for packing.

'How the blazes would I know?' Jeannie said, coming into the kitchen to see.

'It's Kay Magill,' she informed her husband who was still determinedly reading his paper.

'What the devil's she after now?' Jack was nearly at the end of his tether. He thought the days of Jeannie looking after a half-crazed relative at the Orange Tree were long past. The days and hours until they would be safely winging it to the Costa del Sol couldn't pass quickly enough. But he had a terrible sense of foreboding.

Kay hadn't got out of her car. Her head was slumped forward on the steering wheel when Jeannie went out to her.

'Kay, what's wrang? Ye all richt?'

Kay was as white as a ghost. 'She's in a state o shock,' Jeannie said to Jack as she brought her into the kitchen.

'What's happened Kay?'

The last thing Jack wanted was a return to the bad old days when they were imprisoned at the Orange Tree with Jeannie looking after her father. If there was anything they both needed just now it was to get away to the Mediterranean sun. He got a sinking feeling when he saw Jeannie leading Kay in through the door with an arm supporting her crumpled form.

'He tried to kill me last night,' Kay said.

'David did? How come?'

'He came into my room to strangle me. I could see the hatred in his eyes. It was just by the grace of God that I was awake and hiding in the corner of the room.'

'How d'ye know what he was gonnae dae?' Jack said, but Jeannie gave him a look that would have withered him.

'Ye shouldnae be in thon hoose anither night wi him on yer ain,' she said.

Jack saw his holiday plans evaporate. 'We're off on holiday themorra,' he said weakly to Kay, 'so maybe we can …'

'Never mind holidays,' Jeannie interrupted, 'we can go there anytime. We can't leave Kay or David like this.'

Jack walked out of the kitchen in silent disgust and back in again to the sight of Jeannie with her arm round Kay.

'You wait here Kay and I'll go down and settle David.' Then Jeannie turned to Jack and said in a sharper tone. 'Ye comin, or stayin here wi Kay?'

What a choice, he thought. 'I'll come wi ye,' he said, choosing the lesser of two evils.

'Na. Ye'd better stop here wi Kay an make her a cup o tay.'

Jack followed Jeannie into the hall and out the front door to have a not-so-quiet word. 'What the blazes are ye playin at?' he said through his teeth.

'My cousin needs a doctor, an say he gets committed – wha d'ye think'll be in charge o him an the hoose then?'

'Is that what ye're after?' Jack said.

Jeannie gave him another withering look and slammed the car door shut, nearly catching his face. He was left standing there, not knowing what way to turn.

Jack filled the electric kettle from the cold tap in the kitchen. 'Tea or coffee, Kay?' he asked with as much hospitality in his voice as he could muster towards this unwanted intrusion.

'Excuse me?' Kay said. There was a distance in her voice as she stared out through the kitchen window.

'D'ye want a cup of tea or coffee?' Jack repeated. He turned with even a bit of a sympathetic smile, but Kay was ashen-faced and miles away.

'Oh. Nothing please,' she said without looking in Jack's direction. They were both extremely uncomfortable in each others company, and neither had any interest in making an attempt at conversation.

Kay sat on the edge of a wooden kitchen chair, nervously fumbling her keys, as Jack poured himself a coffee and made for the door to the breakfast room.

'You all right, in here?' he said, 'make yourself at home.' She needs a good stiff brandy, he thought, or at least I do.

Kay stood up, walked to the window and stared out in silence as Jack tip-toed out with his left hand under his over-filled coffee mug to catch the drips.

When Jeannie arrived at Kay and David's house, it was as if she had never left the place. David was already at the door, looking up and down street.

'Have you seen Kay?' he asked Jeannie as she invited herself in.

It was not what she had been expecting, for David had been lost in a past world of his own making since his disappearance. But this was a flash of the old David. She remembered the precious and unexpected moments with her own father, when suddenly he seemed to be his old self again.

'She's up visiting us, and I just wanted to check you were O.K.'

'I thought she'd maybe gone off to church or something. Can I fix you a coffee?'

'That would be lovely,' Jeannie said, hardly able to take her eyes off David. She feared the minute she did, she would look back and see her father standing there. The idea that David would be capable of attacking Kay was just as daft as the thought of her own father going on the rampage. But then, he nearly did once or twice when he got really upset. All David needed was a bit of … No! she thought, I'm not getting involved here again.

David was studying her changing body language intently. 'Why did you come back then?' he asked suddenly.

Jeannie thought there was a strange look in his eye, and wondered if something had happened last night that David was covering up.

'Well,' she said as a distraction, 'Jack an me's off on a wee holiday soon an we just wanted to see you before …'

'Ay, Elizabeth. But what did ye come back for?'

A chill ran down Jeannie's shoulder and arm as she realised that David was looking at her with somebody else's eyes. But she felt no fear for she had seen that look before. It was David and old Hugh Magill rolled into one, with a bit of Captain Hugh and Rev. David McGill in there too. Each generation of the Magill family tree bore the fruit of the next, but this seemed to be a tree infected with some sort of hereditary genetic disorder. The fault must have been bound up in the original seed, and it would maybe manifest so long as the house of Magill survived.

'David,' thought Jeannie, 'is mair o a danger tae himsel than tae oniebodie else.' Like the time her father Hugh had charged out into the street and got knocked down. 'It was his own stupid fault,' Jeannie had to reassure the guilt-ridden driver when he came to visit Hugh in hospital. 'He's still fightin the Battle o Athlone and thinks he was hit wi a cannon ball.'

If there was one thing Jeannie had learnt, it was not to humour these delusions by going along with them.

'Ye know it's me, your cousin Jeannie. Jack an me's flyin oot tae Spain in the next couple o days.'

David didn't blink, but his eyes narrowed. *'My father,'* he said, *'took the same line as the King aboot witchcraft.'*

'What aboot you?' Jeannie said, 'Are you goin anywhere nice this summer?'

'Huh!' David grunted, and lost interest in his visitor. He wandered about as Jeannie tried to think of what the next step was. She didn't feel threatened by him, but her doubts grew about Kay being left alone with him.

'Can I get you anything at the shop on the road home?' she said.

'Sure it's Sunday,' David said. 'Where did you say Kay has gone?'

'She's up at oor house. D'ye want to come back up hame wi me?' Jeannie had no idea how to resolve the dilemma.

'Tell her I'm away out for a walk,' David said suddenly. He had been looking out the window and spotted Gumry and the M'Clay brothers gathered at their usual corner spot across the street.

Chapter 13

The Wanderer

It was almost a month after David's second disappearance that Jack and Jeannie M'Clure finally managed to get away to their villa in the Costa del Sol. At least Kay was safe in the house, but there was always the danger that David might turn up suddenly in the middle of the night. One thing was certain, he was still in the locality, dead or alive, for he was last seen by Gumry. He had been seen then heading past the Abbacy ruins into the plantin, with the craas scraiching and birling above his trail.

Over the next week, Gumry gathered as many men together from the lodge as were still at home for the Twelfth holidays. Only about eight or nine were there for most of the first day. It was a dampish Tuesday, and they checked out the best-trodden pads and derelict buildings in the wood. By Thursday the weather had improved, but the band of Gumry's men had dwindled to five in the morning and down again to three in the afternoon.

'It's nae use, Gumry,' Tam M'Clay said. 'If he's leevin, he's hidin, an if he's deid, he's some ither place.'

But he wasn't dead, they knew. Some of the children playing in the plantin had sighted him and chased after him more than once, but he seemed to just vanish into thin air. The weans then came back with bread and jam sandwiches and left them on a big flat stone as 'bait.' But watch as they would, 'Oul Magill' failed to be lured. Of course, the food was gone the minute they left and returned. 'Craas,' said Gumry. The weans looked at each other. 'Oul Magill's deid an turned intae a craa,' they chorused and fled. 'Deid ma airse,' Gumry called after them.

For the first hour of David's wandering he had a purpose that became clearer as he searched through the trees at the back of the Abbacy. The birds – he wasn't sure if they were rooks or ravens but they certainly weren't crows as the locals thought – were trying to tell him something. Or something was trying to send him a message through the birds. When he used to search the graveyard for clues about his family tree, the ravens were always there, screaming at him as if he was on the wrong track. But they didn't live there, they lived in the trees at Easterknowes, an inaccessible part of the plantin just to the east of the Abbacy ruins. That was what he had to find. That special tree. The one mentioned in the old poem that was older than the Abbacy itself. He would know it when he found it, and it just had to be in a special place. Of course, he couldn't tell anybody about his mission. 'He's away wi the birds,' they would only laugh, or 'he's aff talkin tae the trees now.'

The dried-mud paths in the plantin marked out the easy routes through the trees, but the birds stayed well away from them. They were circling over to the left where David had to push through the briers and undergrowth. But he was sure the tree he was searching for wouldn't be near any well-trodden path anyway. David wished he could fly with the birds straight up to their stick nests. What a great view you would have from up there, able to see the world as the saints see it.

There was a strong smell of wild garlic in this part of the plantation. It might have been an old quarry for there were steep, dangerous pits and rock faces here and there. Maybe it was the very place where they got the building stone for the Abbacy. But it wasn't a place for creatures with two legs and no wings anyhow, and that made David all the more excited. It reminded him of the feeling he got when he got into the special collection library in the city. He knew what he was after was within a few feet. All he had to do was focus on the quest and search methodically for the code-breaking clues. The peaceful isolation here, so close to the scurrying streets of Kirkreeba, but so inaccessible, was more calming than any drug he had ever been prescribed. He felt miles away from the hassle of people trying to get him to do things he didn't want to do, or worse still, trying to stop him doing the things he had to do. And then there were the people who pretended to be somebody else, and they would soon be out with their rabid dogs, trying to find him.

The trees here were mostly giant beech trees with a ghostly-grey, skin-like bark. Their massive trunks disappeared into streaming fingers criss-crossing in their through-other reach for the sky. In winter time the rooks' nests could be seen from the Abbacy as dots in the feathery silhouette of the trees against the rising sun. David thought about climbing these trees by considering the progression of possible foot-holds, as only a young boy would, but it only reminded him of his age and human limitations. 'If I had enough faith, I could fly and swoop, like an eagle,' he thought, 'but it's a vicious circle, for I would need to be up there first.' When he saw the massive fallen tree, it was like a sign. How the mighty tree had fallen. It had a different bark. What wind of purpose blew it over? Where did it come from, and when did it start its journey? 'Maybe I can't fly or climb to the tree-tops, but the tree-tops can come to me.' He twisted himself through the tangle of branches, but they were dry, brittle and lifeless. Even at the farthest tip of what had been the top of the tree, he felt nothing. He walked away a few paces and turned back to study the scene carefully. The massive circle of the tree's up-rooted base was the height of a two-storey building. He thought of Jack M'Clure pulling a pint in the Bowling Club, and tried to remember if the pump arm had a big flat base too, like the bottom of a brass candlestick. But this was power on a different scale.

David had never felt fear like it before when he heard a dog bark and voices in the near distance. The rooks were having trouble distracting them, especially the dogs. The only protection he had from this unspeakable swarm of evil was the tree. It was a tower of strength, even when lying flat and unmoved by the wind. Where the roots had torn away from the ground it was like a massive circular shield – an unassailable wall of earth and stones grasped unseen from behind by the tree's claw-like grip of roots. Some of the stones were big, and the crater from which the whole thing had been wrenched was still unhealed. Near the hinge point where a few roots still made contact with the world below, David could see a large flat stone in among the upturned buttress. It looked different, almost as if it was out of a building. Although there were no tool marks on it to suggest it had been wrought, he knew it was significant. His eyes scanned the base of the pit to guess the point that it had been wrenched from. There were other squarish stones there too, but no mortar, so it could have been a dry-stone wall, or the capping off the top of a well. He pulled at one of the other flat stones still in place in the ground, and it came towards him suddenly to the sound of loose earth falling into a dark hole. Another voice called his name, closer this time. David squeezed himself into the underground retreat that he had been led to.

Eventually, the fear and the warning calls of the rooks became more distant. When David's eyes became used to the dark, he realised that this was no natural feature, nor was it the set of a badger or such-like. Instead, the walls were of built stonework and this souterrain, or whatever it was, travelled on in both directions with flat stone caps on the tunnel's roof.

David had never felt excitement like this since he was a boy. He could live here rightly, having parts that lead to the Dear knows where. There was always talk of tunnels and secret underground caves in the village. Rumour had it that there were tunnels for the monks, tunnels for smugglers and even tunnels for the Pechts and Broonies; tunnels running to the Abbacy from the shore and from the Abbacy to the Orange Tree Inn. In the Abbacy ruins there were some collapsed stone-lined trenches that the archaeologists said had been covered waterways. But nobody had ever found the way into the scriptorium chamber under the Chapter House where the old records were supposed to be secured, not until now anyhow. The key to all this was the tree. He had been looking up from here all the time instead of looking down to get, literally, to the root of it all. But he couldn't prove all this just yet. He needed candles, and food.

David had never felt as hungry in all his life. The crows, or ravens, or whatever they were, seemed to be calling him out of his hole in the ground again. It either meant that the pack of demons that had been hunting him must be getting close again, or else the ravens had something more to show him. He felt no sense of danger now, so what could it be? He pushed and stumbled through the briars again to where the commotion was coming from. The ravens were on the ground, so there couldn't be any folk about. They were on a large flat rock the size of a farmhouse table, flapping about and dropping pieces of something white. As David stumbled weakly to the stone, the birds flew off, leaving him great big lumps of bread with butter and jam on. He wolfed the scraps down as if he hadn't eaten for a week. His sense of thrill returned as he realised what was happening and his destiny was rapidly being fulfilled. This was exactly how Elijah must have felt when he too was fed by the ravens in the wilderness. It was just like a sermon he had once preached or heard, or maybe would still give when he completed his mission.

• • • • • • • • • •

The August sun glowed warmly through the shade of the leaves and warmed the hearts of Jack and Jeannie M'Clure as they sat in Orange Tree Square in Marbella, waiting patiently for the café waiter to bring them their bill. This was their ninth holiday in the family villa together as man and wife since Jeannie was given it by her father, and about the only time of the year they felt anything like a couple. Hugh Magill's father had bought it in the 30s as a sort of investment, free of the ties of any will or covenant back in Kirkreeba.

'This is the life,' Jack said. He lifted his wide-rimmed straw hat from the bamboo and cane table and placed it back on his head. 'Fancy another wee drink?'

Jeannie looked up from over her sun-glasses. 'No dear, but you carry on.'

'What's that you're reading?' he asked.

'The book ye got me for my Christmas.'

'Oh. Is it any good? What's it about then?'

'It's aboot this girl that got married an found oot her husband was … ach, it's no the sort o book you would like.'

'You're still thinkin aboot Kay, aren't ye? Look, ye're on your holidays tae get away frae aa that.'

'As a matter o fact, I was thinkin mair o masel, but all the same, I hope Kay's aa richt back hame.'

'*Dos cerveza, por favor*,' Jack said to the waiter, holding up the two empty beer glasses.

'Yes sir, big or small?'

'One big one, and one wee one, *gracias*,' Jack replied. The waiter placed the two empty glasses on a small tray and wove his way back through the tables to the inside of the Orange Tree café. Jack studied Jeannie's face as she started reading again.

'She'll be all right ye know,' he said. 'She's got Gumry stoppin over in the hoose wi her at night, for fear he comes back.'

'Ay, but I hope she doesn't get too dependent on him. She's

the sort needs a man,' Jeannie said.

'Ach, you read too much nonsense in them oul books,' Jack said. 'We'll send her a postcard, an if ye like, ye could even gie her a wee call on the phone thenight.'

'That would be nice,' Jeannie said, 'it would set my mind at rest.'

'An then ye can forget aboot it, an let us baith get on wi oor holiday.'

The postcard was a view across the Orange Tree Square, looking up to the old city walls of Marbella. Jeannie didn't want to mention David in case he had or hadn't turned up. She didn't want to mention Gumry either, for the same reason. She wrote on the back:

'Dear Kay, Hope all is well. Our place is just off this square in the middle of the old town. Everybody here speaks English now, so you would enjoy it if you want to give it a try sometime. There is even a café here called 'The Orange Tree' – now there's an idea! Best wishes, Jeannie and Jack M'Clure.'

Gumry had gone to great lengths to get the lads to cut out the banter about him moving in with Kay. 'It's no like that. She cannae be left on her ain, an we're in separate rooms,' he protested.

That was true enough. Kay was staying put in her own room, and had got Gumry to fix a lock on the door. If David turned up again it would be the end of a big worry in one sense. But what if he just came back in the middle of the night? There was no way that Kay was going to sleep another night alone in that house, even with a lock on the door. For all she knew David might try and burn the house down.

All the same, Gumry went to see his ex-wife Annie to explain the situation.

'Ye can dae what ye like,' she said, 'as far as I'm concerned.'

If Gumry was looking for reassurance from that quarter, he was doubly disappointed.

Kay, surprisingly enough, seemed oblivious to the way in which her co-habitation would be interpreted by those who loved to see the high and mighty fall. It was the furthest thing from her mind, but there were a whole lot of things made Gumry uncomfortable about staying overnight. He knew his way round the kitchen well enough, but it was the strangeness of taking over David's bedroom, even if it was only an emergency arrangement. The awkwardness came to a height in the evening. It was a bit like an arranged blind date – things seemed unnaturally ahead of themselves.

'Want a coffee?' Kay asked as a distraction from Gumry's constant eyeing her up and down. She had been making a sustained effort to avoid eye-contact herself, but could see his minute and constant examining of her out of the corner of her eye.

'It's OK, I'll get them,' Gumry answered, glad of something sensible to say or do.

When he was just about to bring the over-full mugs dripping into the living room, Kay came into the kitchen.

'We'll just take it in here.'

Gumry noticed that she had said 'we,' for his presence in the house had only been justified in the past by his being a workman, and now as a sort of minder.

'It must be a big change for ye, leevin here,' he said. They had talked out every angle of where David might be, where they had searched and what his state of mind was. Kay was glad of the change of subject too.

'Yes, sometimes I wonder why we ever left.'

Kay's answer disappointed Gumry, even in the circumstances. 'There's some good reason for us coming here, but just now it's hard to see.' Kay looked at Gumry as if he might have an answer. Their eyes exchanged a spark that immediately embarrassed them both.

'I'd better go now,' she said and blushed slightly. Gumry felt powerfully drawn to her and studied the back of her hair closely as it swayed softly out of the room. She turned at the door suddenly and caught his eyes on her. 'Goodnight,' she said, without smiling.

Kay knew she wouldn't be able to sleep, so she sat up in bed reading. But she couldn't concentrate. Her mind was in a whirl as she fought with a demon inside her that she had only just discovered. Gumry couldn't settle either. David's room was full of the wrong messages, but his mind kept going over and over every detail of Kay's soft brown-black hair, her lips, her chin, her eyebrows, her shoulders and everything else that might or might not be under her clothing. Fate was so stimulating in its unexpectedness. He analysed every gesture and word and action until he felt sure Kay was going through the same. He imagined her opening her door to an unspoken welcome. He stopped himself thinking further, or at least the awareness that his thoughts were wrong took over. Up he got and paced the room in his bare feet, boxers and T-shirt. Out of the window he could see against the street light that it wasn't raining, although the footpaths were wet. A puddle against the kerb reflected the light with no sign of being disturbed by rain. It was too calm and warm to sleep. It gave him an intense feeling of the importance of that moment in time. Maybe Kay couldn't sleep either.

Gumry opened his bedroom door to see if the light was on downstairs again. It wasn't, but he decided to go down for a glass of water anyway. It would be good to talk some more, for he liked just being with her. As he passed Kay's closed bedroom door, he saw there was a light still on shining through the gap underneath. Quietly he tried the handle, but it was locked.

'Is that you Gumry?'

'Ay. A was just checkin ye had it locked. OK?'

'Yes,' Kay answered after a short pause, 'It's too soon to leave it open, Gumry.'

It was the right thing to say, Gumry thought, whichever way she meant it. Kay slept soundly the rest of the night, safe in the knowledge that Gumry was restless.

There was a brightness in Kay's eyes when she came down to the kitchen the next morning. Gumry had been down early and washed a pot that had been left to soak from the night before. His heart burnt for a breath's length when he heard that Kay was up and on her way down. But there was a cheeriness in Kay's now incredible beauty that unsettled him. Something had changed.

'The post's here early theday,' Gumry said, 'there's a caird here frae Jack an Jeannie.'

'Isn't that lovely? Look Gumry, an Orange Tree Café – in Spain.'

'Ay, A know,' Gumry said, with a growing sense of defeat. Kay was wearing a printed cotton skirt with a tight black belt that made her tummy sit out very slightly like a perfect little pudding. Gumry stood up, sideways on to her in his short-sleeved T-shirt and pushed his shoulders down to display his chest and arm muscles. But Kay was still studying the post-card.

'Do you believe in destiny? That everything that happens in life is for a purpose, good or bad?'

Gumry studied her intently. 'Yeah,' he said, 'when ye look back.'

Kay seemed to have a new confidence. Or maybe she had stopped being scared. It happened when she saw her bedroom door handle turning. The last time she had seen that happening, she was terrified. But last night it was the opposite. Quite literally, it was the turning point, and now the future was suddenly brighter. No matter what, even the twists of life's disasters and coincidences were part of a bigger, exciting plan that was gloriously out of control. It was out of her control anyhow, and maybe her life wasn't wandering aimlessly after all.

Chapter 14

The Summer Fruits

Even in the early morning, the heat was rising from the paving stones as Jack M'Clure flip-flopped alone down to the only shop open at that time of the morning. It was his daily pilgrimage to get a fresh bread roll for breakfast, and he looked forward to doing it himself, no matter what. Breakfast was his task for the day, and Jeannie could organise the rest. The parked cars were all local, for they had that permanent sand-dust colour and that beaten-about look of most fixed objects in the part of Marbella where their villa was. He felt warm inside and out. The heavy responsibilities of the bowling club were a million miles away, and he didn't have to pretend he wasn't watching Jeannie. Here there was just the two of them and they could nyirp on at each other all day long like a normal couple. His drinking habits always changed here too. No spirits, just beer and wine. And Jeannie had only one man here – himself.

In the shop he paid silently for his bread and a jar of local jam. The girl on the till was dark and pretty and knew his name. It didn't annoy him that she always spoke English to him, she knew that he came here to his own place every year, so he wasn't just an ordinary tourist.

'Thank you, Meester M'Clure,' she said with a smile as she came out from behind the cash register to reach him his change and receipt in one hand, and the plastic bag with his purchases in the other.

'*Gracias*, …' Jack had started to say, but she had already turned to the next customer.

Jeannie had the coffee made by the time Jack got back to the villa. 'You know I like to dae that,' he said, genuinely disappointed. But once he had cut a plateful of slices from the bread roll, buttered and jammed one for himself, and set down to take his first bite, the feel-good factor returned. Even the feel of the hard crust scraping the roof of his mouth felt good. Jack took a soothing sip of coffee, swallowed, and let out a satisfied gasp of air.

'Ye know I like tae do the breakfast,' Jack repeated. But Jeannie had too many things on her mind to get annoyed.

'You just get on wi what ye dae best,' she said, '– naethin.'

Jack finished his coffee and studied the inside of his empty mug.

'Dae ye fancy a wee trip oot theday?' he asked in a way that stopped Jeannie in her tracks. The whole point of their holiday was to do nothing. They hadn't visited any of the local sites for years, not since they had friends out to stay with them.'

'I see enough oul churches an ruins an things back hame,' she said.

'What aboot just sellin the bungalow an movin oot here for good?' Jack said out of the blue. There was something he liked about the idea of just the two of therm starting out fresh. Their marriage only seemed to have any life at all when they were out here, away from whatever drove Jeannie to men and him to drink back home.'

'Catch yersel on,' Jeannie said, and busied herself with a thoughtful clearing up of dishes and clothes. As Jack settled himself outside in the morning sun with a book he had been reading for days, Jeannie came to his side with her hands on her hips.

'Were you serious?' she asked in what Jack took to be a half-threatening tone.

'No. Just a sweet little thought, honey,' he said, imitating the way Kay used to talk to David. Jeannie opened her mouth to say something, but the fleeting rush of the sweet thought had been washed away by a stronger wave of disappointment.

They were like a pair of birds in constant, directionless flight. They would only be a real couple again if they were caged up. But they were both too flighty to nest together of their own free will – or at least that's how each of them thought the other one was. The last thing they imagined the other one wanted was to be caged in. That would make their marriage even more of a prison sentence.

But what a glorious, open feeling they both enjoyed here. If they had no Marbella, there would be no marriage. Jeannie came back to the subject like a crow shooed away from a crust of bread. 'The thocht o you wi nae bowls,' she laughed with a forced, questioning grunt.

'Sure there is a bowlin club here in Marbella,' Jack said, glancing up from his book, 'But thon's the last thing A'd want.' He looked back into the book he had opened, but his eyes weren't focussed on the written word. One thing he knew was that Jeannie had no interest in Spanish men, whatever her need was in that direction. Here she even despised the local rich – men and women alike. Jack smiled to himself as he thought of himself chasing the Spanish girls, and Jeannie taking up the bowls.

'Fancy goin doon the Orange Tree Square for a wee coffee?' he said.

'Ye jokin?' Jeannie said, 'You? Coffee?' She smiled properly at him for the first time in months.

· · · · · · · · · ·

David Magill, if he was still alive, was turning into Kirkreeba's scariest man as far as the kids were concerned. But he had competition, for 'Oul Les' had long occupied that singular position.

Les Glynn might have been in his sixties, seventies or even eighties. It was hard to tell, his face was so thin and sunken with skin so tight that there were no tell-tale wrinkles. One cheek had a deep scar that exaggerated the skull-like look of his long thin face, and his colourless eyes were sunk so far back behind his sharp nose that you had to see him straight on to know that he had a squint. His voice was sharp too, if you ever heard it. His company was his own. Even in a crowd, you would think no more of talking to him than you would to a fox or a bird.

His home, 6 Sliddery Raa, was the one you would miss out if reciting the list of inhabitants, for Les was hardly ever seen out and about. The one place he could be spotted regularly was at the Parish church on a Sunday morning. He arrived silently, pushed past any welcoming hand, and took his isolated front seat against the south wall. The only time he ever sat off the wall was the week after a visiting group of foreign clergy had occupied his pew before he arrived. Next week, he was there early and sat on the outside end with his knees pushed forward. When the same group trooped in for their second week, Les sat blocking the pew, knees and eyes pointing rigidly forward. Only he could ignore all the 'excuse me's' as deaf as the brass eagle bearing the bible in front of him.

Les's 'seat' was the only position he held in the Abbacy church, for the idea of him holding office would have been unthinkable. and yet, known only to a chosen few, Les was the hereditary 'Bowle Master' of the oldest closed Order in the country. In fact, it was so closed, and so few, that Les was Master, Secretary and Treasurer all rolled into one. The only other two permanent members were the Chaplin and the Guard Captain, although when ritual was completed and business involved the outside world, the three would permit other parties into the discussions.

Several days after David disappeared, when the biggest numbers of men were out hunting the Plantin for him, Les made one of his rare outside appearances in the village. Despite the warm weather, he was wearing a long black coat with over-long sleeves. In his boney right hand, which could only be seen from the knuckles down, he held a white envelope. Never trusting the post, he delivered it by hand to the Rectory. A week later, the Rev. Cecil M'Intyre made an early morning call at 6 Sliddery Raa. He had a Sunday look on his face, but that was fairly normal.

Gumry left Kay's house by the back door and was still eating a slice of cold soda farl with marmalade on it. He wiped the white flour dust off his face and onto the side of his work jeans. It was back to work, and the hunt for David would have to wait till the evening. To leave by the front door, looking as if he had just been breakfasted by Kay, would only add to the unfounded rumours and assumptions. One minute earlier, and he would have bumped into the Rector, and that would definitely not have looked good in the situation. But, he said to himself, as he quickened his pace to show he had nothing to be ashamed of, all he was doing at Kay's, so far, was helping out till Jeannie got back.

In the few yards he had to walk to get out onto the Lang Raa, Gumry's mind returned to Kay three or four times. It would have only been once, but he kept trying without much success to turn his mind to other things. Then he stopped short and his heart gave a jump. There was Annie sitting in her car watching him emerge from Kay's back door. Watching was not the word – 'glaring', 'steaming', 'disbelieving' then 'devouring the proof with her own eyes' – that would have been more like it. Gumry's heart sank. It would have been better bumping into the Rev. M'Intyre. He raised his hand to wave at Annie, and motioned for her to wait as he crossed the road. He would explain. But Annie sunk the boot to the floor and her car squealed off as angry as a car can get.

This was a turning point for Gumry. His secret fascination with Kay was laid bare, and even his fantasies were exposed. He felt scunnered, for he was sure even Kay didn't know that he was thinking about her all the time. He hoped, and thought maybe from the wee looks they exchanged, that something similar was going on in her mind. It wasn't just physical attraction, and maybe not even that, for Kay was interesting-looking rather than beautiful. But there was attraction. Gumry felt pulled towards her like a strong magnet. Like an irresistible addiction, he wanted to find out all about her opinions, her teenage years in America, in fact everything that made her tick. David might as well not exist anymore. But he did. And the one thing he knew about Kay was that she was completely pure and extraordinarily moral. That was part of what made her so perfect.

A storm was brewing. Cecil M'Intyre really didn't want to get confrontational, but Les Glynn had forced him into it with a special chapter meeting of The Bowle. Dear knows but it was hardly unusual in Kirkreeba nowadays, with fewer and fewer young couples bothering to get married, and plenty of those that did living up and down the street with other partners. But David Magill had a special position in the town as the hereditary steward of the Orange Tree, and 'The Bowle' had a say in that too. If it wasn't enough to have the Magill wife shacking up with somebody else when David was still missing, the situation was made immeasurably worse by her being with one of the Bowle's governing threesome. Gumry didn't yet know that Les and Rev. M'Intyre were about to confront him in formal session.

Kay was oblivious to all the fuss brewing around her and Gumry. She had gone back upstairs before Gumry had left. The minute she heard the back door close, she went into the back study overlooking the Abbacy ruins for her morning devotions. Behind the Abbacy was the Plantin, where everybody believed David was hiding out. She had lost all sense of religion, as far as churchiness was concerned. It was now a matter between her and God. Even her husband was out of the equation now. He was somebody that only existed in her memory back in California. The thing out there in the Plantin was a demon that she had to be protected from. And Gumry was a God-send, unless he started to get other ideas. But what was the purpose in all this? Why was she here, all alone in this corner of the world where even the Lord was suffocating in the trappings of Old Testament religion? If Gumry hadn't been an unrepentant tribal chief she might have seen some answer in his warm friendship. Yes, he was a good supportive friend. Not the sort she would have any sort of romantic attachment with, if she was free, unless of course he changed his views on just about everything. But that would turn him into a wimp, with no strength of character, and the sort of man she never could abide anyway. No, at least Gumry was a real man … Kay stopped herself going down that line of thought. But then the thought returned … and returned again. Where was all this leading her?

Gumry was still out on the Lang Raa waiting for his lift to work in Beggs's builder's van when he thought he heard a scream from inside Kay's house. He didn't need any excuse to go back in, and his heart was pounding.

'What's wrang?' Gumry called to Kay as she came thumping down the stairs half-calling half moaning his name. She was in a right state with her hands flapping as if fending something off.

'Gumry,' Kay said, stopping on the stairs and turning to race back up, 'come up here quickly.'

Gumry followed her up into the back study with his heart racing. She was pointing with an upturned hand out the window, over the back out-buildings and towards the bowling green.

'Look, it's David, out on the bowling green.'

'Where?' said Gumry, 'ye're seein things.'

'He was out there. I swear. He was on all fours like an animal, clawing his way across the green. I thought it was a panther or a big black cat, stalking a bird.'

'There's naethin there. Look!'

'I swear it, Gumry. Please. Don't say you don't believe me. It was him and his clothes were in shreds and black from head to toe.' Kay was shaking all over.

'Sit doon an calm yersel,' Gumry said as he steadied her into a chair with both hands on the rounds of her shoulders. It was the first real physical contact they had had, and Gumry's heart was pounding again. He wanted to hold her trembling body in a close hug for all the wrong reasons. 'If I go doon an tak a look, will ye be aa richt here?'

'Yes.' Her look was enough. That was exactly what she wanted him to do.

'I'll no be lang.'

Gumry went out the back door for the second time that morning, but this time turned down Sliddery Raa and in through the hedge gate to the bowling green. The place was ghostly empty and quiet, neither sight nor sound of a living thing. He walked around just to make sure. The green still had a glistening morning cover of early morning dew along the side where it was still in shadow. Across that part he could see the dew had been disturbed, like a satin pile brushed the wrong way. It was hard to make out. Maybe birds had been flapping about, bathing themselves in the dew. Or maybe a large bag or something had been dragged over the surface.

Back in the house, Gumry placed his hand on Kay's shoulder again, to reassure her, but it was a different look he got this time.

'You think I'm going mad too, don't you?' she said, ready for an argument and in a tone that showed she had regained full control of herself.

'Na. It maun hae been a black plastic bag or somethin.'

'You'd better go on to work now or you'll be late,' Kay said.

He really didn't want to go, but it was more like an instruction than anything else. 'Ye sure ye'll be aa richt?' he repeated.

Gumry was out of earshot and well on his way to work when a second, more terrified scream echoed around the inside of the Orange Tree Tea Room.

That morning in the Plantin, David knew from the minute he woke up that this was to be the day he had to pull himself together and complete the task. He lifted back the camouflage screen from over the entrance to the stone-lined tunnel that ran underneath the upturned root of a large tree where he had made his retreat. There was no doubt it headed in the direction of the Abbacy ruins, but without any light, he had to feel his way along the dark damp moss-covered stones along his right-hand side. In places the roof must have fallen in for the floor was rough and uneven. Other parts he could stand up in and were in good repair. After a painful, groping crawl of several hundred yards, he was sure he had reached the underside of the Abbacy. The tunnel opened out in a large chamber, or so it seemed from the open sound his breathing made. There was no echo. He stood upright and stretched his hand up to check that there was a high ceiling beyond his reach. On the side wall he could feel the base of stone shelves. This was the Scriptorium just where he knew it would be, and he could virtually smell the vellum and leather bindings. Here was the treasury of knowledge he had longed for, where so many questions would be answered when he returned. But he had to press on and find where the tunnel ran underneath and into the chamber below the Orange Tree Inn.

When Gumry left for work the second time, Kay had returned to her vigil at the back study window. There was no sign of anything, and she began to consider the possibility of being mistaken. Only as she was about to go back down to the kitchen did she look down into the back yard. She froze in absolute terror at the sight. A half human form, barely recognisable as David stood almost upright on its back legs below. The hair, beard, clothes and limbs, despite being filthy and matted with dirt, showed that the thing was human, and alive. Kay's apparently exhumed husband was staring up at her with the whites of his eyes showing a certain proof of his living hatred. Then she saw his right hand coming up slowly, like a claw, towards her form outlined in the window. He made a slow scrabbing motion at her and smiled when he heard the scream.

Chapter 15

The Kirkin Bowle

The Kirkin Bowle of Kirkreeba was an ancient wooden bowl, believed to have been carved out ot the wood of an old fruit tree planted by the monks when they first built the Abbacy. It was a treasure of antiquity that had not disappeared into any black hole of a museum store for a very good reason. It had never been lost, hidden or buried in the ground for archaeologists to discover and then the state to claim. Instead, the Kirkin Bowle had, for hundreds of years, been in the private possession of a small guild-like order of the same name. Which came first, the Order of the Kirkin Bowle or the ancient wooden bowl itself, nobody knew. The Keeper of the Bowle was, of course, Les Glynn and apart from Grand Priory meetings of 'The Bowle,' it only emerged from his bedroom for the annual Order of the Kirkin Bowle service at the Abbacy church. A beautifully engraved sketch of it had been published in the *Ulster Journal of Antiquities* in the 1850s, but Les saw it as part of his duty to make sure it was never photographed.

The Bowle itself was a wooden bowl about the size of a pumpkin cut in two, and was the darkest shade of brown this side of black, something like the colour of an earwig, or a *gellick* as they were called in Kirkreeba, and just as shiny and dangerous looking. Dear knows what species of exotic tree it was made of, but it was rock hard and the decoration round the rim could only be seen in the reflection of a light. The one side of the bowl that appeared in the engraving showed the decoration as Northumbrian runes (according to the *Ulster Journal of Antiquities*). This curious script predated the Abbacy itself by several hundred years – or so wrote the nineteenth-century antiquarian who had only access to the engraving, and not the full inscription round the rest of the bowl. 'Noo there's a real mystery,' Les had said with a smile when Jeannie's father had shown him the *Journal*.

There were another two relics that had to be brought together for every meeting of the Kirkin Bowle. The Guard Captain had to bring the Athlone sword, and the Chaplain had to bring the Geneva Bible presented to the Abbacy Church by Rev. David McGill in 1630. The Chaplain kept the Bible in a locked press in the Vestry room along with his clerical robes, and Gumry could get the ceremonial sword anytime from the Orange Hall, where it was kept with a jumble of other regalia. Although the sword was thought of as a ceremonial sword, it was a genuine relic of the Williamite wars. Made about 1645 by the *London Sword and Blade Company*, it was carried by Captain Hugh Magill at the Boyne and fell with him at Athlone in 1691. A careful examination of the Invincible Heroes banner would reveal, among the array of symbols, the Athlone Sword, the Bible and the Kirkin Bowle in a particular arrangement. But despite the accuracy and significance of that arrangement as painted on the Lodge's banner, the Order of the Kirkin Bowle was a completely separate organisation.

In the few short weeks after Les Glynn had convened a special meeting of the Bowle to call Gumry to account over 'his messin aroon wi Mrs. Magill,' a lot of water had passed under the bridge. David Magill had turned up again, alive but definitely not well, Jeannie M'Clure had returned from Marbella to sort out the Magill family mess, and Gumry had got offside the minute Jeannie got back. By the time the meeting happened, Jeannie had helped Kay take David to a custodial care centre, and taken over Gumry's role as Kay's live-in minder.

'Jeannie,' said the Bowle Master, 'ye're maist welcome, the mair ye've been at oor meetins before in oul Hugh's time.'

'I thocht them days were lang gone,' said Jeannie, 'an ye should know Jack an me's decided tae sell oor hoose an leeve in Marbella the year roon.'

'That micht hae to wait.'

Knowing that the last thing Jeannie would do was anything Les Glynn told her to, Rev M'Intyre interrupted. 'With David in hospital and Kay given Power of Attorney, we considered the question of the Orange Tree …'

Guessing what was coming, Jeannie held up her hands. 'No way!' she said.

'No, no,' Cecil McIntyre interrupted, 'We know you had that for years with your father in the same way. We have decided to offer you the absolute ownership of the property, in your own name as Hugh Magill's daughter.'

There was a silence as Jeannie took in what they were saying. Cecil smiled. 'Equal opportunities, you know. If you had been Hugh's son we would never have seen your American cousin here at all.'

'I'm no sayin I'll take it, but is it legal? I know what the legacy says.'

They all looked at each other, and then at Les. 'When it comes tae the Orange Tree, the Bowle's the Law,' he said.

'An what aboot Kay?' Jeannie asked, looking straight at Gumry who hadn't opened his mouth once during the whole proceedings. 'Are ye for throwin her oot on the street?' Gumry looked down and scratched the back of his neck nervously.

'That's up tae yersel,' Les said, 'it's your family she's a freen o.'

Gumry felt lucky to escape from the meeting without having to justify himself. The focus had all been on Jeannie and the fate of the Magill inheritance. It was ironic that he had 'messed aboot,' in Les's sense, with Jeannie on that one occasion that led to his wife leaving him, and had not, strictly speaking, laid his hands on Kay at all. But Jeannie was a one-off tumble, while his heart soared with a sharp pain of pleasure and hurt every time Kay came into his head. Was this the God-damned sin of committing adultery in his heart? No. Gumry kidded himself. It wasn't that he lusted after her. But he had uncontrollable feelings for her that seemed pure and innocent. He cared for her. Yes, that was it, he cared for her with all his heart. And he desperately wanted her to feel the same way about him. When he left the meeting, Gumry felt unexpectedly elated. He wanted to have a heart to heart chat about her future, whether she would stay or go, and hopefully see if he was part of that.

But there was a problem with Gumry's crush on Kay. He was back living in Sliddery Raa, and it was Jeannie that had taken over the live-in stewardship role of minding the Magill house and household. Whether Kay would stay or go was in Jeannie's hands now, after the decision of the Bowle. He needed to speak to her soon, as a spokesperson of the Bowle. He needed to explain carefully and sensitively the situation and support her no matter what happened. He needed just to be in her company.

'We're a right pair, Kay,' Jeannie said as she wrapped both hands round the mug of coffee that Kay had just made for her. 'Both our husbands leevin in a world o their own – mine miles away in a different country, and yours upstairs not knowin what century he's in.'

'Do you still feel married?' Kay said.

'I never did.'

Kay was shocked, and her face showed it. 'Well,' Jeannie said to lessen the impact, 'I mean, I suppose so at the start. But ….'

'I don't feel married any more either,' Kay admitted by way of a sorrowful interruption. 'That man upstairs isn't the man I married. Sorry Jeannie, what were you going to say?'

'Ach, naethin. Did you ever think what it would be like bein' married tae a monk?'

Kay shook her head and looked puzzled.

'One that has taken a vow o chastity and a vow o silence,' Jeannie said with a wee smile.

Kay laughed. 'What does that make us' she said, 'nuns or widows?'

They both laughed and felt an instant bond of sisterhood. After a pleasant silence, Kay turned to Jeannie.

'You know you can stay here as long as you like. In fact that's what I would really love.'

Jeannie smiled and looked embarrassed. She hadn't told Kay that it was now, or very shortly would be, her house. 'It's no' as simple as that,' she said, telling a half truth. 'You know that if David had died, the house would hae gone back tae the Magills.'

Kay looked disturbed at remembering something uncomfortable that she had put to the back of her mind.

Jeannie pulled back with a reassuring smile. 'Tell ye what,' she said, 'we'll dae a swap.'

'What do you mean?'

'I'll stop here an look after your man, an you can take yersel off tae Marbella an take care o mine.'

They both laughed together at the thought. Then Kay looked serious again. 'I don't believe in divorce, you know. Marriage vows are for life.'

'An you an American?' Jeannie said. 'I don't know if I believe in marriage in the first place. As for divorce, I've nae notion o that either.'

'It's different if there are children involved,' Kay said.

Jeannie laughed again. 'Well what d'ye think those two big weans that we've got are?'

It was going to be hard telling Kay that David and her had no right to stay in Kirkreeba anymore. David needed full-time care, whether inside an institution or at home. The best solution would be for them to go back to California, but David had developed a violent aversion to Kay. He didn't recognise her as his wife, but as some demon from his family's past. At the same time, Kay couldn't stand being in the same room as him, and only under the same roof when there was somebody else in the house.

'Is it all right me stayin' on here for a bit?' Jeannie asked Kay by way of avoiding the issue.

'Of course,' Kay said, 'Didn't I say so? And Jack, when is he coming home?'

Jeannie shrugged her shoulders as if she neither knew nor cared. One phone call had been enough to finalise that. It ended up with a two-way ultimatum. Jack was staying in Marbella, and Jeannie could either come out permanently or not at all. She didn't even get telling him that if he did come back, they might be moving back into the Orange Tree. That closed down Jeannie's options, for of the three houses she now owned, the choice was down to the Orange Tree or rattle around in her new bungalow on her own.

Looking after David wasn't half the problem that she used to have with her father. She was the only one could brighten David's face just by bringing him his food or medicine. There was something purposeful and pleasant about that. There was no need to plan ahead, or even think about what to do about telling Kay she was only a lodger in her own home. Until, that is, Gumry knocked at the door.

Gumry was still kidding himself that all he wanted to do was help Kay and show that he cared. Certainly he didn't want to have Kay thinking that he was the reason that the Bowle had turned the house over to Jeannie, and left her with nothing. But it was difficult getting to see Kay on her own with Jeannie there all the time. Dear knows what Jeannie had told her. There was nothing he yearned for more than to be in Kay's company again, talking, reassuring and, above all, being reassured that she hadn't turned against him. His heart was pounding with nervous excitement as he knocked the door.

'Who is it?' Kay called from the back of the house as Jeannie opened the door.

'Just a neighbour,' Jeannie answered, before giving Gumry a silent what-do-you-want sort of look.

Gumry scraped his feet nervously on the ground as if expecting to be invited in, but Jeannie stood her ground.

'A hope ye're no' come tae pester Kay,' she said.

Gumry was devastated. The thought that his affection for Kay was seen in that way by anybody, or – heaven forbid – by Kay herself, was as painful a heartscald as anything he had felt for years. His answer came out before he could think.

'No! I've just come to see how David is.'

Jeannie stood back guiltily to let him in. 'A'll tak ye up, but maybe he's sleepin. He disnae know a soul ye know.'

As Gumry climbed the stairs past the bedroom he had stayed in himself, his knees felt weak and shaky with sick excitement. It was going wrong, his plan to get together with Kay for a heart-to-heart. But he had to save face and had just escaped making a fool of himself. The last thing he wanted was to see David, but if he was in a world of his own, that didn't matter too much.

It was a real shock seeing him in what had all the appearance of a death-bed. If he had been in the hospital ward he wouldn't have recognised him. There was nothing of the old – or rather the young – David left. His eyes were open but unseeing and as colourless as his face. His cheeks were sunken so much that his mouth was permanently open and dribbling as he breathed.

'A hae somebody here tae see ye, David,' Jeannie said, 'a visitor.'

David's eyes moved slowly towards the sound of Jeannie's

voice and Gumry could have sworn there was a faint smile.

'It's me, David – Gumry. Hoo's things?'

David's smile vanished … *as his eyes searched the room.*

'He's tryin tae talk,' said Jeannie as if this was something new.

'D'ye mind me, David, Gumry Caldwell?'

David's eyes seemed to come back to life, as if lighted from behind by a surge of energy. He raised a hand and dropped it. 'Montgomery?' The single word was spat out as if it was a tirade. There was life in the old dog yet. 'Ye've a nerve comin' here an me not even dead yet.'

'Calm yersel,' Jeannie said. 'It's only a neighbour.' She turned to Gumry and whispered, 'ye'd better go on.'

David's head slumped back on the pillow, at the sound of Jeannie's voice.

'So ye dae know folks then,' she said to him. 'I knew there was mair goin on in yer heid than ye let on. An talkin tae!'

'Is this the day I die?' he said.

'Ach, ye're rannerin.' There's years left in ye David.'

Gumry went back down the stairs as sickened as he was when he climbed them. Then his heart jumped when he saw Kay. 'Hi,' he said, 'how's things?'

'Fine,' she smiled with a warm look that made the nightmare visit worthwhile. 'What brings you here?'

'Just seein how David is.'

Kay looked silently at him as her smile faded.

'He seemed to get annoyed wi me bein' there,' he added.

'I know. I can't go into the room without upsetting him.'

'It must be hard on ye. I was just wonderin …'

Gumry was about to tell Kay he wanted to meet up for a chat when Jeannie started coming down the stairs behind him.

'I'll call roon again,' he said to Kay as he opened the door to let himself out. 'See ye.'

For the next couple of weeks Gumry tortured himself, going

over and over in his head every word that had been spoken in the few minutes he had called in at the Orange Tree. At first it was a cold sweat about the embarrassment of it all. Then he imagined the conversations with Kay that he wanted to have. And then he remembered the only thing he wanted to remember – the warm smile. That wasn't the smile of a woman who thought she was being pestered. Even the eyes were smiling. The look in them was full of life, and maybe even love.

'Na,' Gumry thought, 'dinnae turn yersel intae a stalker. Ye maunnae stan ootside Kay's hoose waitin on Jeannie gan oot. Jaist gang up tae tha dorr, an say ye hae cum fur a wee taak wi Kay. Jeannie'll no eat ye. If ye houl on onie lang'r she'll hae forgot aa aboot ye.'

It was another week before Gumry picked up the courage. He knocked the door loudly, and Jeannie opened it.

'Is Kay in? I'd like tae talk tae her a wee minute,' he said eyeballing Jeannie as straight as he dared.

Jeannie smiled with an unexpectedly welcoming smile, pulled the door open and stepped back for him to come in.

'Kay's no here,' she said.

'What dae ye mean?'

'I mean she's no here. She's awa tae … she needit tae get away.'

Gumry's mouth dropped open. 'No here?' he repeated. 'Where's she gone?'

'She flew oot last week,' Jeannie said, enjoying the expression on Gumry's face.

'An David?' he spluttered.

'Oh no. David's stappin here wi me. D'ye want tae come in an see him?'

'No' just noo,' Gumry said. He had given up trying to disguise his feelings, and turned away like a broken man.

Chapter 16

Winter Fruit

GENESIS Chapter 3:

20 And the LORD God said, Behold, the man is become as one of us, to know good and evil. And now, lest he put forth his hand, and take also of the tree of life and eat and live forever,

21 Therefore the LORD God sent him forth from the garden of Eden, to till the earth, whence he was taken.

22 Thus he cast out man, and at the Eastside of the garden of Eden he set the Cherubims, and the blade of a sword shaken, to keep the way of the tree of life.

GENEVA BIBLE, 1599

For every hour of the flight from London to Los Angeles, it took Gumry as many weeks to sort out visas, tickets and sell up at Skiddery Raa. He didn't know if he was leaving for good, or just for a short trip. Even sitting on the plane he still didn't know. That would depend on Kay, providing he could track her down at Orange Grove. Jeannie had been surprisingly helpful, allowing him to store some of his bigger stuff in the old outbuildings at the back of the Orange Tree. That made him uneasy. It was as if she had been encouraging him to go to California, smiling to herself when he asked about Kay, as if she knew something he didn't. Was it a match-maker's smile, or the smug smirk of the opposite? But Gumry had faith in Kay's smile the last time he saw her. That was what was important.

For the first couple of hours of the flight, Gumry's mind was still in departure mode, and it was only gradually that he began to get really excited about the adventure of exploring the other side of the world. He had no idea what to expect, and his TV-based images of America's west coast were little preparation. It was the first time Gumry had travelled so far, and the first time he had flown alone. In the short time zone between the European and the American sides of the north Atlantic, he remembered how the M'Clay brothers had helped him once he had decided to leave.

'The Orange is a warl-wide organisation, ye know. It'll look after ye,' Tam said, 'Where are ye flyin intae?'

Gumry was interested. He had heard of folks going out to America with their Degree Certificates and getting fixed up with jobs and accommodation. 'Los Angeles. That's California, it's no' like Canada. There's nae lodges there.'

'A wudnae be sae sure,' Tam said, as if he was sure.

A week later, Tam had checked out his connections. 'There's an Orange County oot thonner, in California, an it has an Orange City.'

'Wise up, Tam,' Gumry laughed, 'that's where they growe the oranges.'

'Weel,' said Tam, 'hoo come then there's twa Orange Lodges in Orange City then?'

Gumry had been impressed. 'Niver!' he said.

'There's yin problem, but.'

'Oh ay?'

'Yin o them's Masonic, the Orange Lodge o Free an Accepted Masons.'

'That's nae guid tae me. What aboot the ither yin?'

'It's the Elks.'

'The bloody Elks? Who the hell are they?'

'Orange Lodge nummer 1475, o the Benevolent an Protective Order of Elks of the USA.'

'Ye're haein me on. Onyhoo, Orange City is sooth o Los Angeles an I'm headin tae Orange Grove on the north side.'

'Weel,' Tam smiled triumphantly, 'There's a real Orange Lodge in Los Angeles. The Ulster-Scots LOL 1690, California, an it sits in the city.'

Gumry was impressed. 'An somebody'll meet me at the airport?'

'It's aa sorted oot.'

When Gumry finally touched down he had a reality check about the open-arms welcome he was expecting when he arrived at immigration. The slow queue and the suspicious interrogation took any notion of childish excitement away. By the time he got out to the arrivals greeting area, he felt more like a lost child.

All sorts of people were lined up searching the faces of the arriving passengers. Business men in suits holding up paper cards with names printed on them, casually dressed folk scanning for the familiar faces of relatives – and one mountain of a man with man-breasts in an orange T-shirt and a scraggy moustache. He was holding up a piece of cardboard with 'Bro. Caldwell' written on it.

Gumry smiled as he approached and held out his hand. The man only half smiled and half returned the handshake. 'Hi,' he said, 'I'm Frank. My father was supposed to meet you, but I said I would.'

Frank offered to take one of Gumry's bags, but didn't insist when Gumry said he was fine. 'I've my car out in the parking lot,' he said as he waddled breathlessly alongside, talking all the time. It turned out that Frank and his father didn't belong to the Ulster-Scots 1690 lodge, but the 'first' L.A. lodge going back to 1888. The Long Beach Rising Star was the only thing Frank wanted to talk about. He had thin black stubble where there was no moustache, and a bright red, sweating complexion that could be seen through his sparse facial hair. Behind his glasses, Frank's eyes were uninteresting and uninterested. He talked as he walked and talked as he drove. When Gumry asked a question there was a short pause, a short answer, and then a deep 'back to my theme' breath. Frank's agenda was simple. This was a potential new recruit to the Long Beach Rising Star, and had to be kept away from the Ulster-Scots 1690 upstarts.

'Hungry?' Frank said as he pulled his ageing grey Cadillac off the main road into an all-sorts shopping mall. It was still morning, local time, and the thought of a Burger King was the last thing on Gumry's mind. They bought three breakfast deals in a paper carrier bag to take out, and Frank shrugged his shoulders and stepped back when Gumry offered to pay. Back in the car, it soon became clear that they were heading back to Frank Senior and Frank Junior's apartment. Like father, like son, it turned out, for Frank Senior hardly looked Gumry in the eye as he went over the same history of the lodge. The two of them had only one button – for transmit, and none for receive. It also became clear that both Franks assumed Gumry was staying in LA and would hardly be able to wait till Friday night's meeting of the Rising Star.

'I have to get to Orange Grove tomorrow at the latest. Is there a bus?'

Frank looked Gumry in the eye for the first time. 'Orange Grove? Up Fresno direction? Will you get back by Friday?'

'Maybe,' Gumry lied. 'Depends how things go. I've got to see somebody there straight away.'

The Fresno bus ride was a joy, all the more so for being free from L.A. and the two Franks. This was the real California, he thought, once he hit the open countryside and saw the first rows of winter green trees in neat lines. The signs at the roadside told him these were orange trees. If things worked out he would maybe still be here when there were oranges on those same trees. And Kay too – he was just as sure now that their relationship would blossom and bear fruit before the winter set in.

The small town of Orange Grove was not what Gumry expected. He wandered round looking for the town centre but couldn't find it. But it wasn't so small a town that he could expect to bump into Kay simply by being there. Facts were few. Kay and David had lived there, in the town, but he had no address. They had a bookshop in the centre, maybe the main street, wherever that might be. But the one thing she had talked of often was the Crossroads fellowship in a hall behind the Presbyterian Church. That sounded like a candidate for the town centre as well. And one name if he couldn't find her – Pat Mahood, the minister at Crossroads. There were crossroads everywhere, but as he walked past the High School with its green and white bandstand in front, he noticed that the cars were no longer parked in the street, and where they were, they weren't head on to the footpath as they had been back where he got off the bus. And they were all houses with small open front gardens. How did people tell who owned what, with no fences?

Foot-sore, and shoulders aching with the weight of his bags, Gumry turned back to what must, after all, be downtown Orange Grove with its concentration of cafes, churches and shops. In one café which looked out onto a wall mural of orange trees in a plantation, he sat down for a rest. A pretty, dark-eyed waitress came straight over and smiled. Gumry wasn't used to such friendly service, and it boosted his flagging spirits.

'Coffee?' he asked.

The waitress rattled off a list of options, and Gumry replied by repeating the only word he recognised – 'regular.' When she returned with his order, Gumry asked if there was anywhere he could leave his bags while he had a look round the town. 'I'll ask George,' she said.

Within a few minutes a man emerged from the kitchen and engaged Gumry in a quick but targeted interview. 'From Ireland?' was one of the questions. Gumry thought better about correcting him. The last person he did that with in L.A. had thought he was saying he was from 'Austria.'

'I'll take you bags inside, but you'll have to collect them before three o'clock.'

'Thanks,' Gumry said, and paid his bill before leaving.

Where to start? And if he found where Kay's house was, how would he meet up with her without looking like a stalker? He saw a wooden church building and investigated. It was nice, now, exploring the town without dragging luggage about. The notice board said it was an American Baptist Church, but there was another one across the street. It was Orange Grove Presbyterian. A notice said that next Sunday's service was a joint one with the Presbyterian Church in a neighbouring town. A footnote said that the Crossroads Fellowship would still be meeting at the usual time in the back hall. The church stood on the corner of a road intersection, so Gumry walked down the side to the modern hall built at the back. It had its own notice board for Crossroads. That was the first real connection, but he couldn't hang around for four days and then just turn up on a Sunday morning. He didn't want to meet up with Kay like that anyway.

When he got back to Steinbeck's Coffee Shop, the owner was working with a screwdriver at the outside awning. He came down from the chair he was standing on when he saw Gumry, and smiled. 'Were you looking for somewhere to stay?' he asked.

'Not just yet. I was trying to locate a minister here, Mr. Mahood.'

'Pat?' George said, 'Why, do you know him?'

'Well, he's a friend of a friend.'

George smiled warmly and stuck out his hand. 'I knew I could trust you, even if you might have had a bomb in your bag,' he joked. 'I'm George Hamilton. Not a great church-goer, but a good friend of Pat's.'

'Montgomery Caldwell,' Gumry smiled back and shook his hand.

'There's no phone number on the Church notice board.'

'No need. You'll get Pat at any time of the day or night down at the Garden Gate. It's in the old railroad buildings down there. Where the tracks cross the road.'

There was a tall brick wall and two large brick pillars at the entrance to the old complex of railroad sheds that reminded Gumry of the enterprise parks he had seen back home in renovated mills. He just walked in, without being challenged by any security, through the open gateway to a courtyard surrounded by brick buildings, some old some new. The place was busy, with lights and sounds behind the windows, and five or six men about the place, walking from one building to another. A gap at the far end seemed to lead to another courtyard. They seemed different to the people he had seen so far in the town – poor, but not down and out, for they all seemed to be 'working men,' charged with energy. There were few notices or signs about, so he approached one of the men unloading boxes from the back of a van.

'Where would I find Pat Mahood?' he asked.

'He's in the back workshops. Through there and straight on.'

'Thanks.'

'If you want to stay here, just leave your bags beside the canteen. They'll be safe enough.'

Pat Mahood was smaller than Gumry had expected, shorter and thinner. He took his glasses off and put them on the bench he was busy at when the young desk clerk at the workshop door went over to fetch him.

'Hi,' Pat said as he approached Gumry and saw that he was nervous. 'What can we do for you?'

'Are you Pat Mahood?'

'That's me. Is it a job or a bed for the night you're after? Or both, I guess you're from out of town?'

Gumry decided to come straight to the point. 'I'm a friend of Kay Magill's. Do you remember her?'

'The Magills? Kay and David? Of course. I hear that David isn't too well. Have you seen him lately?'

'Ay, he's a lot better.'

'So you're from Ireland? And how's Kay?'

That question floored Gumry. He hadn't even contemplated the idea that Kay wouldn't be back in Orange Grove. 'Fine, the last time I saw her,' he blustered out to give him time to think. Instinct drove him to avoid looking stupid, so he had to pretend he wasn't actually there to find her.

Pat Mahood sensed there was something troubling this young stranger. 'I'm Pat Mahood,' he said offering Gumry his right hand with a smile that said he was going to look after him.

'Montgomery Caldwell,' Gumry said without returning the smile.

'Look,' Pat said, 'let me show you round here, after we've had something to eat.'

Gumry allowed himself to be led towards the canteen, while Pat did all the talking. 'We only eat the best here, courtesy of the local stores. You met George down at Steinbeck's Coffee House? He's a great friend to the Garden Gate too.'

'Anna! Here's a friend of Kay and David's from Ireland,' Pat said to the young helper in the kitchen. Anna smiled at Gumry with the most beautiful brown eyes he had ever seen. 'Anna works with George when she's not up here,' Pat explained.

Gumry liked it here. It was the first time he hadn't felt like an alien since he arrived at Los Angeles. Although Pat was doing most of the talking, he was listening intently even to Gumry's silences. 'How did you like L.A.?' he asked.

'Frankly speaking, it was a strange experience.' Gumry smiled to himself at his own private joke about the two Franks.

'It's one of those strange things,' Pat said, 'I was just thinking about Kay. We got a postcard from her a couple of weeks back.'

'A postcard?'

'Yea, from Spain. Said she was taking a break at some friend's apartment. But you would know all that.'

'Yea,' Gumry nodded, but Pat could see that he didn't.

'Had enough to eat? Let me show you round,' Pat said, standing up to put Gumry at his ease again. There was some reason this friend of the Magills had turned up, or had been sent, and Pat felt that it wasn't just a casual visit.

The Garden Gate complex was a hotchpotch of old railway sheds and some modern infill buildings that were equally industrial-looking. The first enclosure of the two courtyards was large, and around it the largest brick buildings towered over a concrete open space. Gumry liked it here, but it could not be described as a beautiful place. He was surprised at his own reaction – or lack of it – to the discovery that Kay was not here. He was almost glad, for he felt purged of his obsession. For the time being, he allowed himself to be shown around as if he had travelled 6000 miles just to be here.

'This is the life,' he thought to himself as he soaked in the pleasure of the bizarre feeling he had at ending up in this place with these people. Maybe Anna was a significant factor in this change of heart. As they walked back towards the workshops, Gumry had already decided that the canteen where Anna worked was his favourite building.

'These are protected historic buildings,' Pat said with a smile, knowing that the very idea would seem ridiculous to somebody from Europe.

'Kirkreeba has old monastery buildings that's the same.' The idea occurred to him that that the courtyard here was a bit like what the enclosed cloisters of the Abbacy must have seemed in the days of the monks. He liked the sense of security and privacy these high walls offered. He almost understood why the lay brothers were attracted to that life, religion apart.

As they left the workshop, Gumry realised that he actually had skills to offer the place. 'I'm a plasterer to my trade, but I can do most buildin work,' he volunteered unintentionally, as if he was being interviewed for a job.

'If you want a job, you need a work visa in this country, but we could sure use somebody like you.' Pat had a gift for helping folk without them feeling they were being helped. 'But if you wanted to stay here for a bit, you could help out in return?' It was a well tried device with some of the illegal immigrants, but Gumry knew nothing of that.

The inner courtyard, where the living quarters were, was smaller and had a garden in the middle. The minute Gumry saw it he wanted to stay, at least for a few days. 'If you had a tree in the middle it would be like the Garden of Eden,' he said, causing Pat to look sharply at him. They walked past a wooden cross in the centre, but Pat made no mention of it. Both men fell into a shadow of silence as they assessed the other's religion. Gumry wondered if the cross meant that these people were part-Catholic, Pat wondered if Gumry had old-country bigotry as part of his baggage.

'There's not many people get the Garden Gate connection,' Pat said later.

Chapter 17

Relating

REVELATION Chapter 22:

Syne he shawed me the river o the Watter o Life flowin out o the Throne o God, an the Lamb, skinklin like cristal. It flowed doun the mids o the hie-gate, an on ivrie side grew a Tree o Life at beirs frute twal times in a towmond, ae crap ilka month, an leafs at brings hailin til the nations.

The New Testament in Scots
William Laughton Lorimer, 1983

'Religion,' said Anna to her two young children 'is like an orange. It's not what you see on the outside that counts.' She had picked up an orange from the old tree by the well and was holding it up in front of their faces. 'Who wants the outside and who wants the inside?' she said, peeling it expertly with her thumb so that the peel came off in a single, curly piece. Will screwed his face up when his mother offered him the peel. 'That's what the Lord thinks about religion,' she said, sharing out the segments.

It was eight years to the day since Joseph King had died, leaving the ramshackle house outside the city limits of Orange Grove to his son Joel. Back then, Anna and her young baby had been thrown out in disgrace by her cancer-ridden father, to live in the Garden Gate. But the big swap happened when Anna got married and had a second child. Joel moved into the Garden Gate where he worked anyway, and Anna and the new family unit moved into the old house three miles out the county road on the east side of Orange Grove.

Will and his little sister Betty brought the place back to life, just like when Anna and Joel were that age. Anna picked another couple of oranges and took them cradled in her arms back up the wooden steps to the front door. Nobody seemed to worry about the dangers of an open well when they were children. Now it was covered with a timber-framed stretch of chicken wire. But they used to be so silently scared of their father. Now the place echoed to the sound of screams of play. The only thing that hadn't changed was the old orange tree itself.

At the sight of Pat Mahood's pick-up truck pulling off the county road, Will forgot all about oranges and religion. Betty ran to him and took his hand, while Will jumped on his back.

'Hey, you're gettin heavy, Will. Any eggs today?'

Will jumped down and ran into the house to collect the kitchen bowl and bring it out.

'Boy these sure look good,' Pat said, peering enthusiastically into the bowl. The hens now nested tidily in a proper hen-house built for Will by his step-father. 'I guess we'll have to give you a dollar for them.'

It was six years to the day since Gumry first walked into the Garden Gate and got hired as the live-in buildings' maintenance man. Back then he could see straight away that the brown-eyed girl in the kitchen looked at Pat in a special way, and straight away he was jealous. This man had something about him that Gumry wanted. But he couldn't dislike Pat. Quite the opposite in fact, he could see exactly why this man was so attractive. Whatever the chemistry, Gumry at least had purged himself of his crush on Kay. And never for one minute did he regret coming to California.

But sometimes, Gumry would wonder. He might have lost interest in Kay, but he couldn't get over the way Jeannie had let him come all the way to Orange Grove when she knew rightly that Kay was sitting in her Spanish apartment with Jack. It was more than a practical joke. It was malicious. If there was one unresolved issue that annoyed him every time he thought of home, it was why Jeannie had done that to him. He never imagined that it wasn't about himself. These agitated thoughts disturbed him most after he had talked to Pat, defensively, about his background.

'If you want to ring home, use the phone in the office anytime,' Pat had said when he thought Gumry was looking broody one morning. Gumry was just settling into his new job and they had been talking about things. At the start, Gumry knew this guy was a sort of minister, so religion was to be avoided as a subject if Pat would try and raise it. But he never did. Curiosity began to rise, but Gumry's soft probing met with almost no response. Maybe this guy wasn't religious at all, but he didn't seem to be on the make. Maybe this guy just took it for granted that he was an Orange bigot, like Kay did, and that made him feel defensive.

'Religion's at the root o a lot o the world's troubles,' he had said to Pat earlier that day.

'Sure is. Right from the start.'

'You talkin about Adam an the fall?' Gumry said. He was surprised when Pat shook his head.

'Near every war's about religion,' he added, sure that would provoke Pat into giving an opinion on the Irish troubles.

'A good few, yea,' Pat nodded. 'That's the real mark of Cain.'

Gumry was keen to show that he was a thinking man, and that he knew his Bible. 'Cain killed Abel over the head o the ritual o sacrifice. So, it means Adam's two sons were fightin over religion. Right?'

'Maybe it was only Cain that was fighting over religion,' Pat said.

'Ay, but there was a right religion, and a wrong one, even then.'

'There was a right relationship, and a wrong one,' Pat said thoughtfully and slowly, as if considering it for the first time. 'That's the mark of Cain, and that's what can put murder in the heart.'

'Even wi religious folk?' Gumry said.

Pat smiled. 'Well, you couldn't accuse Cain of not being religious, could you? And plenty of wars have good and bad on both sides.'

That was a thought that pleased Gumry, for he was wondering if Pat was thinking of Orange and Green when he was talking about Cain and Abel. He smiled, but his mind was back home.

'Things are different here,' Gumry said sadly.

'It's morning time where you come from. The office is free, go and ring home like I told you, and see how Kay and David are keeping.'

That was not what Gumry had in mind. But he thanked Pat and said 'OK, I think I will.' In the office he pulled out his diary with the phone numbers in it. Kay would be back from Spain at the Orange Tree, but it was Jeannie he wanted some answers from. He found her home number at the bungalow address. The one question he had was, 'why?' But it was only a question between Jeannie and him now. Whatever the reason was for letting him fly to America on a wild goose chase, it was something he was glad he'd done.

The phone rang, and an American voice answered. For a minute, that seemed normal to Gumry, then he asked, 'Jeannie M'Clure?'

'No, I'm sorry, she's not at this address anymore, do you want her Kirkreeba number?'

Gumry was thrown. 'No ...'

'Who shall I say called?'

'Is that Kay?' Gumry asked, realising by now that it was.

Kay was delighted to hear from him. 'Are you really in Orange Grove?' she asked along with a hundred other questions, 'What took you there? Have you met Pat Mahood? What about Anna and Joel King?' Gumry answered some and deflected others, particularly the one about why he had come. 'I'd nae plan, just some sort o curiosity,' he said, 'birds go as far every year under their ain steam.'

'An David?' Gumry asked nervously, not sure if he would be dead or alive. He certainly didn't expect Kay's answer.

'David's been great since we got him out of that old house. He's out in the garden – would you like to speak to him?'

'No, I'm on Pat's phone here. I'll get in touch again.'

'Well write, won't you,' Kay said, 'and tell Pat and Anna to do the same. We're at Jack and Jeannie's place – well it's ours now, but I'll explain some other time.'

As Kay put the phone down her heart stirred again at the thought of Gumry, like it once had when David had gone missing. But it was only a fleeting demon, and easily dealt with. The Lord had healed David from his demonic possession by the simple act of relieving them both of the possession of Orange Tree House. If ever stones could harbour evil spirits, then that place did. She could see why the locals thought the place harboured a haunting of the 'Magill Curse'. Poor Jeannie, stuck there alone now, talking to herself and well past her best. When she did appear at the door, she had a hungry haunted look, much too scary to attract even an occasional 'one-nighter'. But Gumry! Well, that was a surprise. Kay wasn't sure she was pleased that he seemed so happy and settled in her own home town.

Letters and printed photos galore crisscrossed the Atlantic over the four years, and then e-mails and digital photos for another four. There was nothing nostalgic for Gumry in the images of Kay and David in front of their bungalow at 'The Green.' Nor did those of David sitting or working in the 'front yard' make him feel homesick.

There wasn't a great deal of cultural baggage that Gumry held on to from the old world after his first ten years in Orange Grove. But every year, if the 12th of July fell on a weekday, he would ask Pat if he could have the day off. Not that he did much, apart from sit around outside in the sun and wait for people to ask him why he wasn't working. 'Never heard of the Orangeman's holiday?' he would say. The other thing he never lost was the way he enjoyed a wee private joke.

Anna kept up the correspondence with Kay more than anybody else from their home town. 'Aunt Kay', even sent wee Will and Betty presents every Christmas, and her dream was to see the whole family together. 'David is well,' she wrote, 'but not strong enough to fly. Why don't you and Gumry pay us a visit with your children?'

'Gumry is real good, but I can't talk him round to a vacation anywhere outside of California,' Anna wrote. 'Will and Betty would love it – me too. Here's a photo of us all on the new porch Gumry built. He loves to sit out there and watch the kids play, or listen for them when they're inside. That's because he still can't get used to the noisy wooden floors everywhere.'

Kay's dream of having them all come to Europe took a different twist when she tried to talk them all into a trip to southern Spain. With Anna's Mexican Spanish she would be 'a God-send to the community church in Marbella.' But Gumry was even less interested in that.

'This is David in our greenhouse with his treasured tomato plants' the note on the back of one of Kay's photos said. 'Our own little Orange Grove in Ireland!' said another, with 'Look carefully' written in brackets underneath. David was holding two oranges, and the tomato plants were decorated with oranges, somehow fixed to look like they were growing.

Ten and a half years after Gumry first stepped off the bus in

Orange Grove, he could look back with satisfaction at having found his place in the world. The centre of that world was an old well in front of his house, pointing like an inverted spire to the other side of the planet where its maker had come from over a century ago. The tree beside the well had long finished growing upwards towards its Maker, but its roots were still searching in the same direction as the well. This was the heart of Gumry's world now. Where the people he valued most were gathered – Anna, Will and Betty – and where their friends knew they could come and visit anytime they wanted.

It was Gumry's traditional 'Twelfth,' and he was sitting in the late afternoon on the porch, drifting in and out of a doze. Betty had, late in the day, realised that it wasn't the weekend. 'Why is dad not working today, mom?' she asked.

'It's because he's an Orangeman,' Anna said, with one of those little smiles that showed she too liked to tease the children with a private joke.

'What's an Orangeman,' said Will.

Anna looked to check that her man was sleeping, and gathered her two chicks into a conspiratorial, whispering huddle. 'Fetch some oranges from the tree, Will. And Betty, come into the kitchen with me till we get a skewer.' Once the materials were ready, Anna took a long skewer and pushed it right through one of the oranges. 'Let's see if we can thread some string through.' In ten minutes they had all the oranges strung together like an outsize necklace. Tip-toeing and giggling, they hung it over Gumry's forward-slumped head without wakening him. 'Shush,' Anna motioned with her finger. 'Get the camera quick.'

It was the end of August before Kay got her next letter from California, and the photo. 'We got the idea from your one of David in the greenhouse,' Anna wrote, 'no prizes for guessing when it was taken.'

Thousands of cars pass by Gumry's house every summer on their way to the Sequoia National Park without knowing what histories they are passing. But that doesn't matter really, so long as they don't disturb the peace that the Caldwells have found in that spot.

Few, if any, of the hundreds of summer visitors to the Abbacy at Kirkreeba know about the Bowling Club there, or its clubhouse. Inside, on the side wall at the bar, is an array of postcards and photographs. The postcards are mostly from Spain, and the photographs are all of various locals on trips abroad. One of the photos is of a man sitting in sunny California with a beaded necklace of oranges round his neck. At a glance, he could be taken as wearing an Orange collarette, or, depending on your life experience, it might look like a Hawaiian garland. The caption says 'Gumry Caldwell, 12th July, California.'

They say that every picture tells a story. This is the story behind one picture taken a short distance east of Eden.